# FRÉDÉRIC DARD

*PUSHKIN VERTIGO*

# THE EXECUTIONER
# WEEPS

TRANSLATED FROM THE FRENCH BY DAVID COWARD

Original text © 1956 Fleuve Editions,
département d'Univers Poche, Paris

First published in French as *Le Bourreau pleure* in 1956

Translation © David Coward, 2017
First published by Pushkin Vertigo in 2017

This book is supported by the Institut français
(Royaume-Uni) as part of the Burgess Programme

ROYAUME-UNI

1 3 5 7 9 8 6 4 2

ISBN: 978 1 782272 56 4

Text designed and typeset by Tetragon, London
Printed and bound by CPI Group (UK) Ltd, Croydon CRO 4YY

www.pushkinpress.com

*While many of the events in this story are true,*
*all the characters who figure in it are wholly imaginary.*

F.D.

# PART ONE

PART ONE

# 1

What is the saddest thing in the world? For me, it's a broken violin. Which is as may be, but it was the sight of the smashed violin case on the road with the strings poking out of it that got to me most. It summed up the accident more completely than the young woman lying by the ditch, with her fingers dug into the dry soil and her skirt rucked up over her superb thighs. Oh yes, I felt that lifeless violin like a physical hurt. It was like a final twist of the fate which had led me to that place at that time.

I recall that only moments before I'd been thinking about my childhood, prompted probably by the Spanish night which teemed with fireflies and moths that flattened themselves against my windscreen with a dull, sickening, thudding sound… They reminded me of summer evenings long ago when, before I allowed myself to be put to bed, I'd breathe in the sweet fragrance of the old lime tree that stood at the back of our house.

Every evening I'd go outside and spend some time watching the sinister shadows gather against the pale night sky. The air was alive with countless frantic insects which surrounded me and danced the macabre farandole of dusk.

I'd been thinking of the lustrous lost land of my green youth. Like some luminous ploughshare, my headlights traced furrows in the dark. The air was warm and, to my left, the low murmur of the sea filled the cloud-streaked sky. I'd taken a room in a very modest inn beside the sea at Castelldefels called the Casa Patricio which was run by an elderly Catalan couple.

The cooking was no better nor worse than anywhere else, and if the accommodation had proved to be basic, the place at least had the advantage of being located right on the beach. I had a clear view over the sea and it was its monotonous voice which always called to me when the sun transformed it into a great fiery brazier.

The ideal place for a holiday.

And then suddenly everything had changed. Yes, everything, and all on account of that now supine figure which had come out of the night and leapt into the bright lights of my car.

I had slammed on the brakes with all my strength, with all the power at my command. The split second which followed seemed to last longer than the longest years of my life. In a flash, the figure had come into focus; I'd seen that it was a woman and that she was young and pretty.

I'd told myself, in a horrible voiceless scream, that I was going to hit her. In all honesty, there was no way I could have avoided the collision.

The instantaneousness of thought is remarkable. In less than a second I'd asked myself a whole lot of questions about my imminent victim. I found time to wonder who she was, what she was doing at that hour on that deserted road carrying a violin case, and especially why she'd deliberately thrown herself under the wheels of my car. But most particularly I'd asked myself another more secret, more human question: how many sins was I about to rack up with this disaster? At that time of night, there'd be no witnesses to testify that it was a case of suicide.

And then I'd hit her. The collision was actually duller than the impact made by the moths colliding with my windscreen, but the shock of it left my whole being shaking for some time.

My engine must have stalled because everything went quiet, although I'd made no attempt to cut the ignition. Everything around me had gone quiet. I was rooted in a world which had frozen and the sound of the sea no longer reached me.

My first conscious look was directed at my two hands which were trembling. They suddenly seemed alien to me. I made considerable effort to remove them from the steering wheel. Then I flung open the passenger door and leapt out.

The mild evening air began to fill with life again. A flutter of wings eased its return... I saw the smashed violin case on the tarmac and was overwhelmed by the sight of it: it looked like a crushed wooden abdomen spilling its entrails... Something violent, something indefinable rose from the very heart of my being into my throat. I could have wept, but the enormous ball which blocked my gullet prevented me from doing any such thing... I turned and looked at my victim. She was lying at the side of the road, on the bank, in an abandoned pose. It was as if she'd submitted to death the way an exhausted body surrenders itself to sleep.

I bent over her. I was calm again now. I'd never before touched an inanimate body to check whether it was still alive, and I was filled with a sense of immense ineptitude. I had no idea how to set about it. I didn't dare to touch her... My right-hand headlamp bathed her with yellow light which emphasized her blondness. My hand wandered vaguely over her warm body in search of a heartbeat... I found her heart at once, as if it had drawn my hand to it. She was alive! I was filled with a grim, almost painful elation.

Taking extreme care, I turned her onto her back. She was strikingly beautiful. This sudden closeness gave me a shock. Her hair was very long and she had slightly raised oriental

11

cheekbones. Her features were perfectly regular. Her eyes remained closed. Her chest rose and fell in time with her rapid breathing. She gave a low moan.

"Do something!" I told myself.

I cursed myself for dithering. I took hold of the girl by the back of her neck and under her knees. Then, with one heave, I lifted her off the ground. Caught off balance, I almost fell backwards with my load. I steadied myself by holding her closer to my chest then carried her back to the car.

The vanity light was bright enough for me to examine her. Apart from a nasty graze on her left elbow, a few bruises on her legs and a bump on her temple, she appeared to be unharmed... But I didn't dare give a sigh of relief.

Mechanically I turned the key in the ignition. The engine spluttered a few times before starting... I slipped it into gear and a splintering sound came from under the car: it was the violin case. I drove off into the night not knowing exactly what I was going to do with the injured girl. It was the first time I'd been in Spain and I didn't speak the language. That is what dissuaded me from driving her to a hospital in Barcelona. I needed help, and old Señor Patricio seemed to be the only one who could get me out of the fix I was in... Since I was no more than about ten kilometres from Castelldefels and because the condition of the young woman didn't seem critical I decided to carry straight on to the Casa on the beach.

I got there before my victim had regained consciousness. The place was still lit and this made me feel better. The inn consisted of one large whitewashed hall which was used as a dining area. The side looking out onto the beach was mostly window, while in the other three walls was a series of green-painted doors. These were doors to bedrooms which were hardly bigger than bathing cubicles and sparsely furnished with a bed and a chair. These alcoves were more like monks' cells then hotel bedrooms, but life there was lived exclusively outdoors and these cubbyholes designed for sleep made you want to go out and frolic about over the vast beach which bristled with spiny plants.

The staff who worked at the Casa Patricio were seasonal and slept on mattresses laid out every night on the floor of the large communal room. At the back of the dining area a sizeable recess partitioned off by a metal shutter was used as a bar. Old Patricio, drinking from the bottle, was finishing his twentieth beer of the evening. He got drunk twice a day on red wine and then "cured" himself by downing staggering quantities of beer.

He was a short, gnarled old man with long white hair combed straight back and intensely blue eyes. He put his empty bottle down on the narrow counter running round the recess. A deep sigh emerged from between his lips.

He gave me a wink. His drunken face wore a leering expression.

"Had fun in Barcelona?" he said in a thick voice. "You did the *barrio chino*?"

By way of a reply I made a sign for him to follow me outside. Intrigued, he stepped over his employees, who were snoring on their thin mattresses.

I'd left my car door open, so the light would stay on. From the door of the Casa there was a clear view of the injured woman lying on her back on the seat. She might have been some saint or other resting inside a glass shrine. Patricio took a step back.

He asked me a question in Spanish which I didn't understand, then started walking. The wind from the sea plastered his shirt to his sweating body.

He reached the car, stared at the woman then looked up at me. His polite expression had vanished and now as he turned to me his hard Catalan face seemed to have been carved out of boxwood with a knife.

"She threw herself in front of my car on the main road."

He nodded.

"Doctor," I muttered.

"Yes…"

We lifted the woman out of the car… Her clothes were white with dust… Her head flopped down over her left shoulder and the bump on her temple had turned purple.

"You have a room?"

Patricio gave an affirmative nod. He'd taken the girl's legs and was walking sideways towards the Casa. We passed through the eating area without waking any of the staff. With his foot, the old man nudged open the green door nearest the kitchen. Taking great care, we set the injured woman down on the low bed which virtually filled the entire room.

Patricio examined her thoroughly. He undid my victim's printed blouse and ran his thick fingers sedately over her chest. The sight revolted me, and with a quick movement of my arm I pushed his hand away.

"No! Doctor!"

"Yes… I'm going…"

And off he went muttering vague words under his breath which were doubtless not very flattering to me. A moment later I heard the roar of his two-stroke motorbike as it tore along the bumpy road. I dropped onto the foot of the bed, my legs giving way with the after-effects. It had been a terrible shock to the system and I was finding it hard to deal with. My hands had begun to tremble just as they had at the moment of impact.

Inwardly I sent up a prayer that there'd be no lasting consequences for the young woman... What was worrying me was the fact that she was so deeply unconscious...

I left the room and, as I passed the bar, I grabbed Mister Gin's bottle. Mister Gin was an English tourist so named by the other guests staying at the Casa Patricio because he drank the equivalent of a full bottle of gin every day. He'd make an appearance after lunch and old Patricio would begin serving him continuously until he closed up for the night.

Usually he finished the bottle. But that evening he'd left about a wine-glassful which I drank straight from the bottle.

Patricio returned a quarter of an hour later, accompanied by the local doctor. And a strange sort of doctor he was too. He looked more like a street hawker with his thin canvas suit, his look of exhaustion, wire-rimmed glasses (one arm of which had been mended with white cotton) and his unshaven cheeks.

He crouched by the bed to examine the patient. First her head... then the rest of her body... As his examination progressed, he proceeded to remove her clothes. I felt my cheeks redden because she was pretty and had a good figure... When he'd finished, he gave a nod.

"No serious damage," he said to me.

He cleaned her wounds and bandaged them up. He asked me for fifty pesetas which he slipped into his pocket with the quick gesture of a money-loving man.

"*Hasta mañana!*"

"See you tomorrow, doctor."

15

I considered his diagnosis a trifle hasty and his treatment somewhat basic, but I said nothing. When he'd gone, I tucked the woman up then felt her brow. It was cool and she was now breathing regularly, as if she were asleep.

"Bed!" old Patricio said to me and showed me to my room.

"What about the police?"

He frowned. The word made him nervous.

I watched him shift his weight from one foot to another. He smelt of sweat and the rough red Spanish wine had left his lips covered with a purplish film which flaked at the corners of his mouth.

He was probably thinking about the *carabineros*, Spain's border guards, who patrolled the beach each morning and always dropped in for a drink at the Casa.

"*Mañana*…"

"*Mañana*" would be time enough to take stock… No one hurries in Spain… It is a country that lives off its former glories and has yet to be gripped by the heady fever of progress.

I gave one last glance at the young woman lying on that monkish bed with her long fair hair for a pillow. She was something like a character out of a legend… There was mystery behind that delicate face.

I dragged myself away from my ruminations. I could have spent the rest of the night gazing at her, the way a sculptor of genius contemplates the recumbent figure on a tomb which was born of his chisel.

*Mañana!*

Yes, tomorrow… Tomorrow, perhaps I'd know…

**2**

It took me a long time to get to sleep. Outside on the beach, Tricornio, the Casa's house dog, kept barking at the fishing boats whose riding lights out on the sea marked a sort of luminous frontier. I was riven with anxiety. In the darkness of my tiny room I relived the various phases of the accident... I couldn't manage to surrender myself to sleep... The same series of events kept running through my head, and opening my eyes wasn't enough to break the sequence: it was something that went on happening inside me. I saw the bright triangle of my headlights, the grey road, the hedges of lentisk and the shape—I knew at once it was human—which, I knew not why, was leaping out at me. My entire body became a brake, a mass of muscles bracing itself against the inevitable. I felt the shock... And again, as horrible as the never-endingness of hell, the same question would arise in my reeling brain: had she been badly hurt?

The crushed violin case... Details I'd paid no attention to but which my senses had registered now came flooding back through the dense darkness... I saw the black pegs still attached to their strings strewn over the tarmac... The velvety-purple sheen of the case...

I eventually dozed off before finally sinking into a heavy sleep at the bottom of which the Mediterranean boomed.

Then, as happened every morning, it was the bustle of the hotel staff which woke me. There were three of them. There was Tejero, the bone-idle waiter; Pilar, who washed the dishes; and Pablo, a rather simple-minded adolescent who did everything and nothing and whose main usefulness lay in soothing the nerves of old Patricio when he'd been overdoing the manzanilla.

When they were awake the three of them sang heart-rending flamencos as they cleaned the hall. Usually I made myself scarce and went for my first bathe. When I opened my eyes that morning, I found that my anxiety was intact. All the same thoughts were there, lying in wait for me.

I leapt out of bed and hurried barefoot to the anonymous woman's room.

The staff, who hadn't been told anything, watched me with surprise.

"*Amigo?*" Tejero asked me.

"*Si…*"

I opened the door.

She was awake and sitting on the bed with her back against the plaster of the wall examining the grazes covering her arms.

At the sound I made as I entered she looked up and for the first time I saw her eyes.

They were tawny and filled with flecks of gold. They added intelligence to her good looks, which is truly the finest gift that can be bestowed on a pretty face.

She stared at me. The sudden appearance in that tiny room of a man in pyjamas must have left her nonplussed. I smiled at her as I tried to work out where to begin.

Of course, I came out with the most banal words that only an idiot like me could have found.

"Did you sleep well?"

She didn't reply. Her blazing eyes burned into my very soul. In them I saw a burning need to know.

"I... It was me driving the car that knocked you over last night... How do you feel?"

Suddenly I realized I was speaking to her in French and that consequently there was every chance that she didn't understand me.

The hotel staff were standing motionless in the doorway, staring with surprise at this new guest they hadn't seen arrive... Pablo's pale stupid face irritated me. I pushed the door shut with my foot. Above the head of my victim was a skylight which allowed the sun to shine in. In the bright light her skin glowed in a most extraordinary way. I'd never seen skin so tempting; it seemed so soft and warm that I wanted to stroke it.

I sat down on the bed.

"Do you mind?"

She held me with those tawny eyes, but her anxious expression relaxed and she seemed calmer now.

"What happened to me?"

I give a start. She'd just spoken in a clipped voice, in French, and with no trace of an accent.

"You're French?"

"French?"

She thought about this for a moment, as if she didn't quite understand the meaning of the word. Then she nodded.

"Yes... French..."

The accident seemed to have affected her memory. Again I felt a surge of anxiety.

"You don't remember?"

A spasm shook her whole body. Each word passed through a filter before reaching her understanding.

"No."

I could see that she bitterly regretted not being able to remember. The need to know was like a physical ache.

"Last night on the road… You…"

I hesitated. I couldn't very well bring up the subject of her failed suicide attempt. The word "accident" seemed more appropriate.

"I bumped you with my car. You really don't remember?"

"No…"

"Where do you live?"

She raised one hand to her head… Her forehead was furrowed with the effort.

"I don't know."

"Do you live in Spain?"

She started. Then in a disbelieving voice she stammered:

"Spain? Why in Spain?"

"You really don't know that we're in Spain?"

A flicker of amusement appeared in her eyes, but it was fleeting.

"You're joking!"

"I'm not joking… We're in Castelldefels, a few kilometres south of Barcelona. Barcelona. Come, doesn't that ring any bells?"

My throat had gone dry. If she couldn't remember that she was in Spain then she must be in a bad way.

Again, in a voice that barely carried, I stammered:

"Barcelona."

"No! Is this true?"

Suddenly, without anything to lead up to it, she began to sob. She cried the way a small girl cries, without any of that instinctive embarrassed need to hide her tears.

"What happened to me? What happened?"

I put my hand on the back of her neck. It was warm and even smoother than I thought.

"Don't upset yourself. It's the shock… It'll wear off… Wait a second, let's try something different, I'm behaving very insensitively."

She stopped crying. Her face was suddenly lit up by hope. She waited expectantly.

"Are you in pain?"

"My leg hurts a little… and my head… There's a buzzing in my ears."

"Yes, you've been badly shaken… I promise you it'll pass off… No need to worry, I'm going to take you to see a specialist in Barcelona."

That got her attention.

"Barcelona!"

Clearly I was going about this with all the subtlety of an elephant.

"What's your name?"

She shook her head.

"But I…"

"Go on…"

"I don't know!"

What I felt at that moment was something approaching anger. I couldn't accept that fate was letting this happen.

"What do you mean, you don't know? Everybody's got a name… no one forgets their own name! For God's sake! Try and remember!… Your name! What's your name? Durand? Martin? Boileau?… Those are names, do you understand? Me, for example, my name's Daniel, Daniel Mermet."

My outburst scared her. She lost the trust she had in me.

Still, she wasn't crying. She just lowered her head as if she felt the shame of it.

That left me feeling crushed.

"I'm so sorry... I'm so dreadfully sorry that you're here like this on my account."

I stroked her hair... I could feel the bump on her temple with my fingers. She winced with the pain.

"Does that hurt?"

"Yes..."

I examined the bump. It was angry, purplish, with a small round hole in the middle of it. It was through that tiny hole that her memory had absconded.

"I'm thinking that you must have papers with you... When people are abroad they don't go around without some means of identification..."

Her clothes were there, on a stool, in a heap. I felt them. They contained nothing except a handkerchief with an "M" on it.

"Your first name must start with 'M'. Could it possibly be Marie?"

She repeated it:

"Marie... Marie..."

That wasn't it. I knew it by the way she pronounced the name. She wasn't familiar with it.

"All right, we'll try another... Take your time... Maybe Mariette?"

"No..."

"Close your eyes... That's it... I'll call you by different names that all start with M. Perhaps you'll get a feeling that you know one of them. It's not Marcelle?"

She opened her eyes.

"My name isn't Marcelle."

It was stiflingly hot in the room. I opened the skylight and the sound of the sea grew louder. And the sound of the heat too… To my mind, it's the loveliest sound there is… It crackles, it fizzes, it's euphoric… It hums… It keeps changing, it excites.

"Listen, Martine…"

There was something slightly sinister about this game… It made me feel depressed… What was the sense of it? If we had to go through such mental gymnastics to come up with a first name for her, then if we went on using the same technique we'd never succeed in reconstructing a valid past for her.

"Marguerite?"

"No…"

"Madeleine?"

"No!"

The further we proceeded with this roll call, the fainter and more despondent her noes became.

"Marthe?"

In the end she made do with just shaking her head… Then she closed her eyes again, worn out by the prolonged effort. A moment later she was asleep. I tiptoed out of her room and closed the door, lifting it slightly to stop it creaking.

# 3

I felt rather lost in the large, cool hall where the other guests—all Spanish—were having breakfast. I'd have liked to discuss the situation with someone capable of speaking my language, but the rare people who did speak French at Castelldefels spoke it very badly. Conversation with them was invariably limited to comments about the food.

Old Patricio was busy getting outside a hefty collation, punctuating each mouthful with a gulp of wine which hardly touched the sides. He directed it in a thin jet of deep purple straight down his gullet from one of the orifices of a two-necked *porrón*. When he saw me he gave a nod.

"The *señora*… She sleep well," he said with satisfaction.

"*Si*…"

"French… Could have tol' you," he said.

He looked relieved.

"Really?"

"*Si*…"

I said nothing. The two *carabineros* who patrolled the beach three times a day walked in, rifles slung over their shoulders, their three-cornered hats set at a jaunty angle, leering at the bare legs of the swimming-costumed women holiday-makers.

Old Patricio raised one hand by way of a greeting. The entire local population feared these border guards like the plague and paid obsequious court to them. They both sat down at his table and Tejero brought two glasses and a full bottle at his usual funereal pace.

Patricio started talking to them. He spoke slowly. He was telling them all about my adventure of the previous night, because the men kept giving me curious glances. The word *francés* cropped up frequently in what the old man was saying. When he'd finished, he forked a fearsome slice of garlic sausage into his mouth while the men walked to the door of the woman's room and opened it.

I followed them, impelled by an obscure need to protect her. The two policemen remained in the doorway. The cloth of their uniforms gave off a sour odour of sweat and grease. They lingered there watching the woman, without saying anything. They turned and looked at me reprovingly then closed the door again.

"*Papeles!*" growled the younger of the two who wore a narrow stripe made of wool.

I didn't understand.

"*Pasaporte!*"

I gave a cooperative gesture and went off to fetch my passport. They stared at it as they did at my international driving licence and my car's regulation green card.

"The *pasaporte* of the *señora*?"

"I haven't any… I don't know who she is…"

With the aid of much hand-waving I explained that she'd lost her memory… And I told them about the accident… They gave a vague gesture which I interpreted as being reassuring. They wrote down my identity details in a grubby notebook and then went back and emptied their glasses. Patricio gave me a wink. Then the two *carabineros* went out onto the scorching beach and I watched as their long, grotesque shadows rippled over the undulations of the sand.

"Is ver' good," said Old Patricio.

He explained in his own way that the *carabineros* didn't give a tinker's damn if I'd run over a French woman. As long as there was no corpse making the public highway untidy.

I gave a sigh and went for my shower in the communal washroom. I shaved and swapped my pyjamas for a checked shirt and jeans. My easel, which was leaning against a wall in my room, beckoned to me. Almost mechanically, I slipped the strap of my paint box over my shoulder.

I exchanged a questioning look with the innkeeper's wife, who was coming out of the accident victim's room. Señora Patricio was a fat, comfortable old body who, as far as I knew, had only one fault: her habit of always making food that was swimming in oil.

Putting both hands together, she leant one heavily jowled cheek on them to indicate that the patient was sleeping. Her husband had told her all about the accident and she was full of it.

I left the Casa... That morning, the sea was a deep green which put me in mind of the Adriatic. My painter's temperament reclaimed me. I walked down the beach and set the three legs of my easel at the water's edge, where the sand is damp but out of reach of the waves.

I didn't paint the sea but, instead, the row of picturesque buildings which formed a kind of multicoloured garland all the length of the coast.

After all, I had plenty of time to decide what to do about the young woman. First I needed to wait to hear what the doctor said... That afternoon, I'd go to the French consulate in Barcelona. There they'd know how to advise me. The identity of my victim shouldn't be too difficult to discover. She must have had papers to enter Spain. She must have come in

26

somewhere... Doubtless other people had been with her and they'd have reported her disappearance.

Anyway, there was no call to get too worked up over it... The main thing was not having her death on my conscience.

I started to paint. Now when I paint, nothing else in the world exists except my palette spattered with colours and the special universe which I create in two dimensions.

What's more, my subject absorbed my full attention. It was an inspired decision that had brought me to Castelldefels. Despite the infernal heat, despite the sea, despite the scattering of turntables which churned out *fados* and flamenco, and despite the luscious colours, all the sad fragility of Spain was there, set out before my very eyes. The characteristic small houses lining the beach exuded an indefinable air of quiet desperation, and the bathers too seemed despondent... In fact, wasn't the whole tone of the landscape set by them? The bathing costumes of an old-fashioned cut, too long, lacking in grace... And the faces, serious even beneath the smiles... Worried and resigned... Undernourished...

I was painting the way an athlete strives for the perfect performance. My heart was pounding and my temperature rising. It was a good feeling yet it saddened me. It was both exhausting and exalting... I trembled as I squeezed my tube in search of the ideal blue I was looking for... The joyless blue of Spain... an intense yet faded blue which, unlike all other blues, reflects no hint of peace.

Now and then bathers would stop near me and stand in silence as they watched me work. I had long since stopped being bothered by inquisitive eyes. I no longer felt remotely awkward knowing that I was being watched because, over the years, I had succeeded in blotting out anything that was not

27

my art… In those moments of intense concentration, my life doesn't escape the confines of the canvas rectangle in which I find fulfilment. That rectangle is inviolable territory, and there I rule like an absolute master.

Even so, I eventually noticed one persistent shadow at my back. After adding a touch to my canvas which pleased me enormously, I turned round. It was her. She was there with nothing on her feet, her hair awry, her blouse torn and bandages around one knee and an arm.

When I saw her I put down my palette.

"You! But… how…"

She looked rather pale. Her skin was still as velvety, but its colour had faded, like a fabric which has been kept in a drawer for too long.

"It was the old man in the shirt… He showed me where you'd gone."

"Do you speak Spanish?"

No… but… he understood that I wanted to see you…"

It was silly but that gave me a lift. That she needed to come and find me made me feel exceedingly good.

"You don't feel ill?"

"No… I'm hungry…"

"Come on, then, we'll go and get something to eat."

I put my tubes and my brushes back in my paint box.

"Are you a painter?"

"Yes…"

I wanted to ask her a whole string of questions so that I could check how bad her amnesia was now. But I didn't dare.

"You've got talent," she murmured.

She didn't take her eyes off my painting.

"You think so?"

"Yes... Especially your blues!"

I was struck by the remark. I took her by the shoulders and looked deeply into her eyes.

"Who are you?" I murmured in a low whisper.

A hazy film dimmed the directness of her gaze.

"I don't know... Are you sure we're in Spain?"

"Surely you must have worked that out?"

"Yes..."

She looked up towards the top of the beach. There was the Casa Patricio with its long white façade, green shutters and the large red splotch of the billboard advertising Coca-Cola.

"It's beautiful. Don't you think so?"

"Yes."

"So this is Spain... It's somewhere I've always wanted to go."

It came out just like that. I took her by the arm.

"So you do remember?"

"No, why?"

"You said you always dreamt of going to Spain."

She dug deeply, reaching inside herself for some hint of a previous life.

"No, I can't remember anything... I *feel* that I always dreamt of visiting Spain, that's all... I can feel it, I can understand it as I stand here looking around me."

I jerked my easel free of the damp sand. I held it away from me to protect the fresh paint on my canvas... I put my other hand around the waist of... of X, to help her to walk.

# 4

She ate with a healthy appetite, even a certain relish, which contrasted strangely with her reserved manners.

It struck me that perhaps she hadn't had a meal for a long time... I thought about the violin case. I thought it odd that a young woman should be wandering around in the middle of the night on a road in Spain with all she had for luggage consisting of a violin case. Maybe she was part of an orchestra which was playing a season on the Costa Brava? She'd probably lost her job and that was what drove her to commit such a desperate act.

"Where are you from?"

I had asked the question straight out while I went on eating. I wanted to try and force her memories to the surface by suddenly asking questions in the most natural way.

She replied in the same easy manner, with her mouth full:

"From..."

Then she stopped abruptly... It was as if someone had punched her in the face. She swallowed the piece of bread she had in her mouth with one gulp.

"It's awful," she sighed. "I don't know any more... Everything's hazy... it's all grey."

Two tears pearled on her long eyelashes; I watched them roll down her cheeks, with the more than depressing feeling that there was nothing I could do...

Helplessly, I muttered:

"Come on, don't cry, I'm here..."

That probably sounds conceited, but to be honest I could find nothing more comforting to say. She went on eating, her eyes fixed on her bowl of coffee on which the buttered bread she'd dunked in it released small gleaming beads, like stars.

I looked at her sadly. To judge by her clothes, she came from a middling background, or at any rate she was someone who wasn't particularly well-off. Her skirt and blouse were the kind sold in department store sales… That gave me the idea of checking the labels on her things. It might give me a lead.

"Do you mind?" I said by way of apology as I turned back the collar on her blouse.

She was as docile as a doctor's patient. I found the small rectangle of material and the name of the maker. It said: "Établissements Février, Saint-Germain-en-Laye, Seine-et-Oise".

"Do you know Saint-Germain?"

She hadn't heard. She was lost in her thoughts as she ate.

"Listen: Saint-Germain-en-Laye… Does that mean anything to you?"

Her faint "no" came down like the blade of a guillotine.

I left it at that.


When she'd finished a substantial breakfast, Pilar, who washed dishes, took her off to the communal washroom. Tejero came and started clearing the table. He pointed to the chair vacated by my nameless victim and made a screwing movement against the side of his head with his forefinger.

"*Loca!*"

I just gave a shrug.

The other guests gave me disapproving glances. I have no idea what they thought of my attitude, but it certainly didn't tally with the small-minded standards of that part of the world.

All of them irritated me. Even Señora Rodriguez gave me the cold shoulder. And yet she was ostracized by the small clique

31

at the Casa Patricio because every weekend a gentleman came to see her, and it was never the same one twice.

I walked out of the communal hall. Old Señora Patricio was preparing fish for lunch, as she did every day. She didn't return my smile... And the half-witted Pablo stared at his feet as I passed by.

Good God! What on earth were they imagining? That I regularly ran women over because I enjoyed making them lose their memories so I'd have them in my power?

Furious, I went to get my car out of the bamboo lean-to, and while I waited for the woman to complete her ablutions I smoked a Spanish cigarette which had the acrid taste of burnt grass.

When, with her blonde hair tied up at the back of her neck and her fresh new complexion all aglow, she came out again into the sunshine that beat down on the Casa, I got quite a shock. I wanted her to stand still so I could start painting such a marvellous subject there and then.

I gave a brief toot on my horn to attract her attention. She raised her bandaged arm over her eyes to shade them and saw me... I opened the passenger door for her.

"Get in..."

"Where are we going?"

"Barcelona."

In a half-choked voice she repeated:

"Barcelona."

I sensed that she was having difficulty getting used to the idea that we really were in Spain.

"We're going to sort out this business of who you are."

"How?"

"By putting the French consulate in the picture first, and then the Spanish police... Dammit, you didn't just drop out of the sky. And even if you had, someone must have been there when you did!"

She gave one of her woebegone smiles, which grieved me more than her tears.

"Is what's happened to me unusual?"

"You don't see it very often, it's true, but there have been other cases like yours, you know..."

The car bounced over the poor, bumpy road which led through a pine wood to the main highway. As we went we raised a tremendous cloud of yellow dust. The car changed colour. It now looked like a camouflaged wartime army vehicle. The billowing dust stung our eyes and made us cough... But finally we came out onto a tarmacked surface.

The hedges lining the main road were in flower and birds chirruped on almost every side. Implausible, elderly vehicles rattled along the highway.

"It's very quaint," observed my victim.

She was interested in everything and looked avidly around her at this way of life that was so different from ours.

I was thinking that at exactly that moment, twelve hundred kilometres from here, in Saint-Germain-en-Laye, someone was perhaps thinking of the woman and what had become of her...

I glanced across at her. The sun which lit up the whole of one side of her head brought out the incomparable flesh tints of her face. I told myself that when she was happy she must be much more than merely beautiful.

"I'd very much like to paint your portrait."

She turned and looked thoughtfully at me.

"Why?"

"Because you have an interesting face..."

"I do?"

She seemed genuinely surprised.

"You do indeed! You have a face that inspires an artist... It could be painted or written about or set to music... I don't know if you understand what I'm saying..."

"I see what you mean but I don't agree that my face is what you say."

"Oh, but it is..."

We passed a pig farm, and the most appalling stench of over-ripe pig muck almost made us gag. Then we came to the turn-off for Barcelona airport. Instinctively I kept looking across at the other side of the road in the hope of seeing the remains of the violin case. But I saw nothing. Nothing stays less still than a road... Many people had driven along it since the accident. The first to pass by had crushed the remains of the instrument and the tyres of the rest had obliterated all trace of it.

We drove into the Plaza de España. Workmen from the highways department were clearing up litter into small dust carts drawn by donkeys. Others were hosing down the pavements, and an agreeable odour of damp heat hung over this part of town.

At a junction, a policeman in white uniform and helmet was directing the traffic by doing his best to imitate a robot.

I pulled up level with him.

"Do you speak French?"

"No."

"Do you speak English?"

"Yes."

Behind me a cream-coloured tram was sounding its horn. With a wave, the cop told him to be patient. I asked him where the French consulate was and he told me.

My passenger pointed to the bullring on the Plaza de España.

"Is that the bullring?"

"Yes."

"I pictured it differently... More... more Roman! It's a bit like an amphitheatre, don't you think?"

That was exactly the impression I'd had when I arrived in Barcelona.

"True."

"Have you ever been to a bullfight?"

"I go every week."

"Is it any good?"

"If you like it, it's great, and a painter can't not like it..."

"I'd like to see a bullfight..."

"There's one tomorrow in the Plaza Catalan. I'll take you."

My promise came as a complete surprise to me. There I was, with this creature of the night which I was trying to restore to the place in society which it had occupied before it threw itself under the wheels of my car... And now I was making plans for her future! I wanted to paint her portrait, take her to bullfights...

She thought for a moment. We were driving through streets which were not crowded. Ten o'clock is virtually dawn in Spain...

"Do you earn your living from painting?"

"Yes... It's rare, I know! I was lucky: a big-time collector took a shine to my work last year. A gallery got interested in me and gave me a contract. Oh, it's not untold wealth but it gives me a comfortable sum each month which allows me to paint without having to worry about the price of steak and the gas bill... So I travel... I'm drawn to the sun... It's the only true light..."

"Like Van Gogh?"

It was scary. She couldn't remember her own name but she remembered the name of Van Gogh... What psychiatrist could have followed the loops of her subconscious?

And then we were parking by the consulate's flagpole. I told her to get out of the car and we walked through the portico where a policeman on guard duty was nonchalantly rolling himself a cigarette with black tobacco.

I told the woman to stay in the waiting room while I saw the consul. I wanted to speak to him without her being there so that I wouldn't need to choose my words carefully. The consul was a middle-aged man who you wouldn't have been able to tell from a Spaniard if you met him in the street. He was courteous and unbending and had the peevish air of a man who starts his stopwatch the moment you step through the door of his office.

"What is your business?"

I told him what had happened in some detail. He listened without interrupting, though he occasionally glanced at his wristwatch.

Eventually, when I stopped talking, he gave a slight shake of his head.

"This doesn't come within my province," he declared.

"I'm sorry?"

"There is no proof that this person is French."

"But I would remind you that she speaks only French and that her clothes were bought in the suburbs of Paris!"

"These are circumstances which cannot be said to constitute proof."

"But I would point out—"

He cut me off in a voice that wasn't accustomed to contradiction.

"Fill out an accident report form and send it to your insurer."

I began to lose my temper.

36

"I don't think my insurer will be interested in identifying her. I assume she isn't alone in this world... There must be people who are expecting her!"

"Contact the local police... No, wait a minute, I'll do it."

He picked up the receiver and dialled the number... Someone answered the call... He began speaking in Spanish. From time to time he'd cover the mouthpiece with one hand and ask me questions:

"Where exactly did the accident happen? What is your name? Where are you staying? Can you describe the woman?... Are you prepared to take her to hospital?"

I gave detailed answers to every one of his questions except the last, to which I replied with a very curt "No".

The consul went on parleying for some considerable time, then he slammed the receiver down hard on the cradle.

"Well, there it is, all we can do now is wait. If there is anything new, the local authorities will be in touch..."

"I'd prefer to have the young woman looked at by a good doctor. Could you possibly recommend one?"

He wrote down an address on a sheet of paper torn from a pad.

"I hope he can speak French," I growled.

"No need to worry, he qualified as a doctor in Paris..."

"Excellent. I'm most grateful to you."

The diplomat escorted me as far as the waiting-room door. When we reached it he stopped in his tracks as he caught sight of my victim. It hadn't occurred to him to wonder if she might be beautiful, and she quite took his breath away.

"Goodbye, sir," I said.

Then I took her by the arm and led her out of the building. Basically, I wasn't too unhappy with the short shrift I'd been given, because I was in no hurry to be parted from her.

# 5

It was only when we were sitting in the car that she dared to ask questions.

"Well?"

"I filled out a report form for the consulate. The consul informed the police... It's quite likely the authorities will follow up any reports of missing persons that are made to them. They'll probably circulate all hotels giving them your description... We'll have to wait..."

"But what shall I do in the meantime?"

"You can pose for me. I told you I wanted to paint your portrait..."

She didn't say anything and I drove her to see Dr Solar without uttering another word. She saw the brass plate fixed to the iron gate of the Spanish-style house and she got the message. But not a muscle in her face moved.

A maid already running to fat opened the door for us. I told her we'd been sent by the French consul and that we wished to see the doctor as soon as possible—I'd prepared a few Spanish phrases, which proved adequate. She showed us directly into the doctor's luxurious consulting room and we sat down side by side, both feeling oppressed by the same sense of unease. A good quarter of an hour went by before the doctor arrived. He must have been in the bath because when he came in he smelt of shaving soap and still had traces of talcum powder on his earlobes. He was a robust old man with white hair and sallow skin. He spoke French fluently, but with a strong accent.

Once again I summarized what had happened. He seemed to be interested by my story. He began a thorough examination of the young woman's head.

When he'd finished he took me to one side.

"I don't think it was the trauma that caused the amnesia. And judging by that fairly superficial wound, the blow she took to the head was relatively light... No, I think this woman was already suffering with nervous problems or else it was the shock of the accident that triggered a mental disturbance..."

"So what's to be done, doctor?"

That was what he'd have liked to know too. But he didn't try to pretend otherwise.

"We're faced with a case that leaves medicine groping in the dark. I think she needs peace and quiet... If in time her brain doesn't start to spark by itself we'll try electric shock treatment."

"Could you give me your honest opinion, please?"

"Frankly, I have no opinion. Perhaps her memory will come back gradually. Obviously if she were to be with people she loves or in familiar surroundings, she'd recover more quickly..."

In a word, we were no further forward when we left his clinic than when we went in.

We set off on the drive back to the Casa Patricio.

"It's permanent, isn't it?" she asked me as I turned off the main road onto the dusty track.

"Nothing is final... Don't worry about it... Just go on living your life..."

She nodded in agreement. She was resigned.

A strange vehicle drawn by a donkey was parked outside a cluster of well-to-do houses. On a cart festooned with faded garlands was perched a mechanical piano decorated with sad-looking illuminated designs which was playing old tunes. A man dressed in clothes that had seen better days was grinding them out with an effort that looked too much for him. On the back of the cart his wife was tucking up a very small baby in a cot. It was covered with weeping scabs. She had long black tangled hair and an expression more tragic than I've ever seen on a human face.

The music coming from the mechanical piano was even more pitiful than the conveyance it stood on. It hung swirls of despair on the pompons decorating the ears of the donkey.

I stopped the car. My passenger's eyes were brimming. Her distress made me feel better because it proved to me that she was capable of feeling pity. That other people's misery could move her to tears at a time when she herself was deserving of pity brought a lump to my throat.

"I'm beginning to learn a lot of things about you," I murmured. "Already I know that you're pretty and that you're kind. Those are the two main qualities that a painter and any man can hope to find in a woman."

# 6

I parked the car in the shade of the bamboo lean-to.

"Come on…"

She followed me. I felt slightly awkward as I walked into the Casa. Fortunately, the guests were out on the beach and the Patricios were both busying themselves in the kitchen. The air stank of hot oil. I was well on the way to losing my appetite entirely in this country.

The young woman remained standing in the middle of the dining area watching Tejero setting out plates and cutlery on the questionable tablecloths. He pretended not to see us.

I touched my victim on the arm.

"Your clothes are torn and covered with dust. I should have bought you some more in Barcelona… We'll do that tomorrow… Meanwhile, I'll lend you a pair of denims and a shirt. They'll be too big for you, of course, but we're not going anywhere special…"

I think the get-up amused her. I happened to have a pair of very narrow black jeans and a striped linen matelot top… Naturally, both were much too big, but their very size gave her an artistic look which suited her very well.

Female coquettishness reasserted itself. She stopped at the misty mirror in the bar to tie up her hair.

"Would you like me to start on your portrait straight away?"

"Yes."

She seemed to like the idea… Her cheeks flushed with pleasure…

I went off to fetch what I needed from my room. I stowed my current canvas behind my bed and selected another clean one, of middling size.

There's nothing more terrifying for a painter than a blank white canvas. It's like a window that opens onto infinite possibilities. A window from which the most disturbing metamorphoses may emerge.

I knew of a quiet spot, far from the beach, in the pine wood. The sandy soil was strewn with sticky pine cones and the cicadas were making a devil of a racket.

I brushed the pine cones away and pushed the legs of my easel in deep so that it was low enough for me to work kneeling down. To my mind, that is an ideal position from which to paint. It puts you in a state of intense engagement which is required for intense concentration. Kneeling, ultimately, is the physical equivalent of concentration.

"Sit down on the sand."

She sank down onto the dusty ground. Have you ever seen a piece of silk drop onto the floor? As it falls, it describes the most elegant arabesque. That's exactly how it was with my model...

"Do I have to stay absolutely still?"

"Oh! Yes... but it doesn't really matter..."

But she did sit without moving, her face half turned to one side, looking at me out of the corner of one eye.

I chose a fairly large brush and worked black into it.

For me, a painting always starts with black because in my opinion black is the foundation of the completed work. I do a preliminary sketch in large bold strokes and then colour is hung on that frame and slowly overlays it.

From the first touch I had her exactly. I tell you frankly, it was one of those small movements of the hand which distinguishes real artists from the rest.

My model simply took up residence inside that white rectangle. It was her to a T... She was almost more real than her real self. These were her features, her high cheekbones, her deep, inquisitive eyes, her slightly mocking mouth... and also her air of quiet melancholy, her gentle disillusionment.

I was in a world of my own. I lost track of how long I spent overlaying one colour with another. I was no longer aware of anything: not time, not place, not even of my subject as a human presence. What I set out to show was what I could see in her. She surrendered slowly, easing herself out of her own personality to become what I wanted her to be. I no longer separated my creation from my model. I took a human being and spread it out on a surface which had no limits.

Eventually I became aware of a heaviness in my arm and cramp in both my legs. I put my brush down and stretched out full length on the hot sand. As I lay flat on my face, arms outstretched and feet pointing outwards, I listened to the distant pulsations of the earth as a man listens to the beating of a human heart. All the heat of that Spanish summer had leeched into the fine, slightly greyish-white sand. It seeped into me slowly.

I was aware of a scuffing sound beside me. It was her coming closer to me. She sat cross-legged and the shadow of her hand moved across the ground like the shadow cast by a bird. I felt my head being stroked. She had laid her hand on my hair and her fingers were moving gently.

I sat up. I reached out one arm to pull her close to me. She went slack against my chest and then stopped moving. Her body was even warmer than the sand. We lay perfectly

43

still like that for some time. I thought of nothing. I was happy…

And then she murmured.

"How about 'Marianne'?"

Believe me if you wish, but it wasn't she who realized that it was the right name: it was me. I knew it was hers by the way she said it.

I put one hand around the back of her neck and, bringing my mouth close to hers, I muttered:

"Marianne!"

I saw two tears roll down the sides of her nose.

"My name is Marianne…"

"How did you come back to you?"

"I don't know… I think it was because I was lying close to you. I just wanted you to call me by that name."

"It's a very nice name."

I looked at her lips and wanted to press mine to them. But carnal desire formed no part of my need. I kissed her. She kept her lips closed. They were firm and tasted sweet.

"Marianne!"

My love for her began at exactly that moment, just as a race begins when the starter pulls the trigger of his pistol. It was the strongest, the most joyous kind of love because it was offered to someone who'd just been born. I was living the dream that all men have: of loving a woman without a past. A woman to whom we represent a new start.

For her everything had begun on the previous evening. What had happened before that belonged to a completely different Marianne who'd died beneath the wheels of my car.

# PART TWO

# 7

I'll say nothing of the days that followed except they were the most wonderful of my entire existence. Every minute of my life with Marianne in the sun-drenched paradise of Castelldefels was pure enchantment. She was unfailingly sweet and tender. I can honestly say that we lived practically cheek by jowl for a fortnight. We went to bullfights and to late-night restaurants on the coast where the reddening leaves of the trees smouldered with innumerable multicoloured light bulbs. We went for trips up into the scrubby hinterland and along the sea as far as Sitges.

I felt that the Creator had entrusted me with the role of beginning the world afresh with this woman. She'd sprung from the night, just for me. And I kept her fiercely for myself. But she wasn't my mistress. We exchanged chaste kisses and moments charged with passion, but we never went as far as consummating our love, and that scared us. Of course it was what we wanted, but only half-consciously, and it was that which scared us.

There would be time for intimacy later. I knew it would most certainly bring us fulfilment, but I also knew that it would spoil something that was unique. Thanks to her, I had the amazing good fortune to rediscover my adolescent innocence. I had become brand new again with her. She'd given me my chance, and it was truly a gift without price.

Eventually we were fully accepted at the Casa Patricio. I think the other guests were touched by our love and made allowances for its unconventional nature. The question of

Marianne's identity became less and less of a problem for me. On the contrary, I began to fear that one morning I'd see someone turn up who'd reach out to her and call her by her name... Who had she been with when she crossed the border? Her parents? Friends? A lover?... A husband? She wasn't wearing a wedding ring, though that didn't mean a thing... But she behaved like a single girl and most certainly I couldn't imagine her as a married woman... Moreover I could never glimpse anything of what I called "her previous life" because I preferred not to think of such things.

But whether it was husband or parents, boyfriend or lover, she hadn't come alone and there were people looking for her. They would go either to the French consulate or to the police, and be directed to Castelldefels... But nothing happened, and the days went by in the golden peace which I've described.

I had finished her portrait. From a painterly point of view, it was first rate. Yet I didn't like it, because with this particular canvas something strange had happened. I had succeeded in capturing Marianne's most unguarded expression so well that I could read her character better in my painting than in her face. Now, in the come-hither look in her eye with which she stared at me I detected a bizarre glint which quite disconcerted me. There was a sparkle in it which didn't seem to belong with the rest of her: it encapsulated a level of sustained attentiveness which was almost disturbing in its intensity.

To escape it I had packed up my canvas in a cardboard sleeve and stowed it away in the boot of my car. But from time to time I would go out and scrutinize it in the unforgiving light of day. Immediately that right eye would strike into the very heart of me and make me gasp. If I hadn't been so pleased with my work, I believe I would have gladly destroyed it.

But the original soothed the hurt. The glint in Marianne's eye was definitely there, but it didn't have the same effect. The very opposite. It was reassuring and I never wearied of basking in its loving glow.

"I love you, Marianne."

Her cheek would flush pink. I would kiss the wind-blown hair at her temple and put an arm around her waist which I could feel pulsating beneath my fingers.

Everything about her delighted me: her excitement at the bullfight when the blood would rush to her face, and from her mouth would issue a stream of rapturous cries. Her endless daydreaming at my side as I painted her... She would wriggle in the sand and grab it in handfuls. She would watch it run between her clenched fingers in a thin golden trickle while the wind from the sea would blow it this way and that, like smoke.

Sometimes she would suddenly jump to her feet and come to me, to inspect my canvas. She loved my painting and talked about it with exceptional intelligence. She was totally alive to its elongated forms and strong colours. She understood the poetry of my subjects... She was a wonderful audience! One afternoon, immediately after our siestas, I was on the beach painting, with my face to the sea which was swarming with crowds of unlovely people. Marianne had just been for a swim and was lying on a vast striped beach towel of many colours getting a tan. There was a light breeze and the water smelt strongly of sea salt. The cracked voice of old Patricio sang out:

"*Señor francés! Señor francés!*"

He could never remember my name. I turned round. I saw him on the narrow terrace of the Casa waving a small piece of white paper.

"*Correo!*"

I put my palette down. There was an unpleasant tightness in my throat. Marianne, looking magnificent, was dozing in the blinding sun which picked out grains of quartz and pieces of seashell in the sand and made them sparkle.

"Mail!"

I practically never received letters. This had to be about Marianne… I walked towards the Casa Patricio with heavy steps. I sensed danger, a threat to my happiness.

The old man stood watching me. For some time now there had been an unpleasant smile on his face whenever he spoke to me. He couldn't understand the behaviour of this amateur dauber who fell madly in love with women he knocked over in his car.

"*Correo!*"

"*Gracias.*"

I gave a sigh of relief. The letter had been sent from Paris. I even recognized the envelope, which was from my gallery. I opened it with a fingernail.

I started reading. My first reaction as I took in its contents was elation, because Brutin, the director of the Galerie Saint-Philippe, informed me that my work had been noticed by a rich American art patron and that a large exhibition of my paintings would be held in two months' time in Philadelphia. Here was virtually fame! Or if not that, it was a giant step on the road to fortune. Brutin wanted me to go back to Paris immediately because it meant going to the States where, he said, "my youth and good looks would be winning cards to play in the publicity game."

I turned round to face the beach. Marianne was standing in front of my easel. She was staring at my painting, motionless, with her head slightly inclined to her right.

Suddenly my euphoria evaporated. What would happen to her? We'd have to go our separate ways. You cannot take people across borders when they have no papers. I suddenly realized that the dream we were living really was only a dream, and that it had brought me only the illusion of happiness.

This state of affairs couldn't go on forever. Marianne would need, officially, to become someone.

I walked down the beach towards her. The sand burned my bare feet. It hurt but was not unpleasant. Marianne was observing an insect with bluish wings that had settled on my canvas. One of its wings had got stuck in a patch of wet paint and the poor creature was vainly waving its legs while it waited to be rescued.

Marianne took hold of it carefully between her thumb and forefinger. She gave a sharp tug and the wing tore off and remained stuck to the canvas. She opened her hand and inspected the mutilated insect. It turned in circles in her palm, dragging its other wing like a sabre.

I took a step forward, dismayed by her casual cruelty.

"Why did you do that, Marianne?"

She jumped. She hadn't heard me coming. For one brief moment I saw her eyes flash with the terrible glint which so disconcerted me in her portrait. And then it was gone.

"But, Daniel, it was messing up your landscape."

I said nothing. I held out my letter to her.

"Is it… about me?" she asked.

"No. They want to send me to the United States, for an exhibition of my paintings."

"And you're not keen?"

"I'd like to go, yes… but with you."

She didn't understand. Then she gave a delighted skip and flung herself against my chest.

"You want to take me with you?"

I looked at the ground.

"No?"

Anxiety made her voice falter.

"To go to the United States, Marianne, you have to have identity papers."

"Ah yes, of course…"

She stepped back. Her lovely face resumed that air of sadness which sometimes made my heart stop.

"I understand," she stammered.

She turned and stretched out on her towel. She lay down flat, with her face directly on the sand.

"I understand," she said again. But this time she was saying it to herself.

I dropped down beside her.

"Well, I'm going to discover your identity, because that is what we have to do!"

She didn't react.

"Did you hear what I said, Marianne? I'm going to do something about it now… I'll find out what your name is…"

"You'd really do that, Daniel?"

"I'm going to do it! And I won't hang about, there's not much time…"

I packed up my easel and paints.

"Wait for me here, I'll be back for dinner."

"Where are you going?"

"Barcelona!"

"Shall I come with you?"

"No, I'd prefer to go by myself. I need to think... and when I'm with you, I can't think about anything else."

She kissed me. The kiss tasted of fruit, of woman. I realized I couldn't live without her. If I couldn't clear up the mystery surrounding her, well, I'd give up all thought of going to the States... If it proved impossible to arrange things so that she could leave Spain, then I'd settle permanently in Spain. I was prepared to make any sacrifice to keep her.

"All right, Daniel... I'll wait for you."

She lay down again on the burning sand. She settled herself comfortably, as though preparing for a long wait.

# 8

I thought very hard as I covered the few kilometres which lay between Castelldefels and Barcelona. The first priority was to speak to the consul again, to ask if there was some way of enabling Marianne to return to France. Once we were there, it would be easier to trace her identity. First, because she was French, and then because the avenues open to us would be more effective than those available to the Spanish authorities.

But the consul's view was even more disappointing than it had been on my previous visit. He based it on logic. There is no way anyone can cross a border without papers. Except illegally, of course. If I decided to go down that route and Marianne were to be arrested, she risked ending up in an internment camp because she couldn't provide proof of her identity.

I told him that we could lodge an official application with the Spanish government simply by putting the case to them. Since Marianne was so obviously French, there was no reason why she should be refused the right to return to her native country.

The senior civil servant shook his head. Of course, we could always lodge an application but the result would be very long in coming and very uncertain. Besides, it wasn't in our interest to draw attention to Marianne since her situation was irregular... Finally, the last valid objection: even assuming that everything went well with the Spaniards, we'd also have to smooth things over on the French side, because in the final analysis there was nothing to prove that Marianne really was French.

"But," I said to the consul, "we can hardly leave this woman without an identity…"

"Circulate her description in France. She may be on the Bureau of Missing Persons list."

"I'll do that. Thank you."

I left feeling very unhappy. It was patently obvious that I had little to hope for from what are normally referred to as "the authorities". Marianne's case rather scared them, all of them, French and Spanish. I'd have to fend for myself.

I parked my car by the kerb of a well-shaded street, walked to the terrace of a café on the *rambla* and sat down. Dense crowds flowed past like melting tar. It was very hot and my shirt stuck to my body.

I was suffocating. My throat hurt and I was probably running a temperature… Brutin's letter rustled in my pocket, the letter that in a single instant had wrecked my happiness, the letter that had dropped a terrifying reality into my lap.

I ordered a beer and closed my eyes. People who disappear are rare. And those who aren't found are rarer still. For these there are only two possibilities: either they're dead or they wanted to disappear.

By losing her memory, Marianne had left a social vacuum which could be recovered.

I drank my foaming beer straight off. It made me feel thirsty. I ordered another.

I sensed I was about to have an idea. Something crackled in my brain the way the radio crackles before it starts transmitting.

I had one important clue. Her clothes came from Saint-Germain-en-Laye. If she'd bought her clothes as near to Paris as that, then she must have lived in that town or at least in that immediate area. I told myself that Saint-Germain was in the Seine-et-Oise *département*, so there was a good chance that the passport on which had Marianne had entered Spain had been issued by the Versailles prefecture.

I stood up and gave the waiter a hundred-peseta note. From where I sat on the terrace, I'd noticed that there was a camera shop next to the café. Until that moment I'd never bothered with photography, but now circumstances had awakened my interest.

As I was leaving the shop, I saw a blind man playing the violin near a newspaper stand. He'd placed his open case on the pavement in front of him and charitable souls were filling it generously with small change.

The sight reminded me of the night of the accident. I'd often thought of the violin case lying smashed on the road… But I'd never been able, so to speak, to associate Marianne with it.

Yes, I'd found a lead I could follow… Marianne had lived each day that passed with total and utter peace of mind. Never once had I tried to winkle her past out of her fogged-up memory. Perhaps the time had now come to start working on her to that end. After all, Marianne held the truth I wanted to recover in herself. It had to be released from its dark night…

I crossed the *rambla* and walked along a foul-smelling alley which led to the *barrio chino*. You can get everything in that squalid part of town. Girls, abortionists, drugs, second-hand dealers, grocers, shops selling stuffed crocodiles…

I had no difficulty finding a maker of stringed instruments who without too much haggling let me have a very respectable violin for a thousand pesetas.

Now that I'd acquired these objects, all I had to do was to set off in pursuit of Marianne's past.

# 9

In the few intervening hours she hadn't moved… I found her lying in the same odd position she'd adopted when I'd left. She was turned on one side, with her knees up and her head on her outstretched arm. Her hand was buried in the sand. His skin was lobster-red.

"You'll give yourself sunstroke!" I exclaimed.

She sat up. There was an odd look of disbelief in her eyes.

"Ah, it's you," she murmured. "It's you, Daniel!"

She hiccupped.

"In the flesh, my darling… It's me. You seem surprised!"

"I was afraid that you wouldn't come back."

"What an idea!"

"Yes, now that I'm looking at you, I realize I was being stupid."

I kissed her for being afraid because her fear proved how much she loved me. I hungered for her body. I clasped her to me so hard she could hardly breathe… Her skin was on fire, burning up… Her mouth was burning too… I was overwhelmed by a wave of impetuous desire. I needed to have her at once. The danger hanging over our love suddenly gave me an acute sense of what total love is…

"Come on!"

I dragged her off towards the Casa Patricio.

In the slow time between lunch and dinner, Tejero was lolling in an armchair on the terrace with both feet on a table. He was reading a romantic novelette whose cover featured a badly executed greenish-coloured drawing…

He watched us over the top of the book as we came in, and I read in his dark eyes a reflection of my own desire. He'd twigged straight away what I was up to and why I was dragging Marianne into the Casa in such a hurry. He who always had a smile on his face now looked serious, with a hint of longing in it.

In the hall, Mister Gin was walking up and down with a drink in his hand, mulling over old memories of the tropics… He didn't even see us making for my door.

It wasn't particularly cool in that small room, but the temperature was noticeably lower then on the beach.

Marianne lay down on my bed.

"It's nice here…"

I took off my sweat-soaked shirt.

I lay down beside her on the red coverlet… She was breathing deeply. I put one hand on her breast. She turned her head and looked at me. Her eyes were pools of infinity. Flecks of gold swirled in them like bubbles in a glass of champagne.

I wanted to say "I love you".

But I couldn't speak the words. My throat was held in a grip of steel and I could hear my heart racing. It filled the whole room with its muffled beating.

But she knew all right.

"I love you too… You'll never leave me, Daniel, will you?"

"Never!"

"Promise?"

"I swear."

"But what if you can't take me with you?"

"If I can't take you with me, I won't go."

"But you'll have to go back to France, won't you?"

"I'll go to renew my visa, but even if I have to take out Spanish nationality, I'll stay with you."

I slipped off the strap of her bathing costume. It was full of sand, which scattered all over the coverlet. There was sand in her blonde hair too.

I kissed her. Her lips were salty from the sea. Her skin was salty all over. The top of her costume had worked loose. I pulled it down and her breasts spilled out. They were as hard as marble.

She muttered: "So you really do want me?"

"I want only you, Marianne. You're my whole world."

I pulled her bathing costume down some more. It was stuck to her thighs and she got out of it by jiggling her hips. It was green and like a serpent's skin being shuffled off. I ran my hands over the sensual line of her back. My hand slid slowly across her flat firm stomach. Then something turned me to ice. I snapped out of my ecstatic mood and stared at the totally unexpected imperfection which I'd felt beneath my fingers. It was a scar, and it spoke louder than any medical certificate: it was the sort of scar that can only be left by surgical childbirth.

I was devastated. Until then, whenever I wondered who might be waiting somewhere for Marianne, I'd thought of parents, a lover… I'd never imagined it might be a child.

"What's the matter?" she sighed.

There must have been a frown on my face, because she propped herself up on one elbow. The tip of her left breast brushed my cheek.

I closed my eyes.

"Nothing, Marianne, I love you…"

Then I took her the way a man might kill himself, with a terrible determination to escape the unbearable.

# 10

When we'd come round—for the fierceness of our embrace was tantamount to a loss of consciousness—the sun had gone from the small skylight and the air had acquired the mauve tinge which in those parts usually precedes the coming of night.

She was lying on the bed, breathing hard, dazed, with her long hair plastered over her cheeks and one arm dangling over the side like a broken branch hanging from a tree. I felt drained. My prostration had placed me beyond fear. For what I'd felt at the revelation that Marianne was a mother was first and foremost fear. The physical fear of losing her. If she got her memory back, she'd start thinking about her child. And then the maternal instinct would assert itself and I would no longer matter to her. If I discovered her identity, her husband would claim her... In a word, I'd taken on a task which could prove fatal for me. I was forging a sword destined to fall on me alone.

"What are you thinking about, Daniel?"

"I'm fine," I lied through my teeth, "I wasn't thinking of anything."

"Everybody is always thinking about something or somebody."

"So what are you thinking about?"

I almost shouted the question. She drew her hand back over my chest, her fingernails gently scratching the skin.

"I was thinking about us, darling... I want you to promise me one thing..."

"What?"

"It's stupid, so promise first…"

"All right, I promise…"

She fell silent.

"Well, out with it!"

"If you should ever leave me, Daniel, I want you to kill me first!"

It didn't make me laugh. Love, when it is genuine, is always close to death. Because love is basically a yearning for the absolute, and nothing is more absolute than death.

"I promise."

"Thank you. You know, you mean everything to me. *Everything!* This must be the first time ever that a man has meant so much to a woman. I believe dogs feel for their masters what I feel for you!"

"Don't say that!"

"But it's true, Daniel! Can you imagine what's going on in here?"

And she tapped her head.

"One morning I open my eyes on the world. I'm a grown woman. I think, I exist, and yet I'm nothing… or rather I'm just a living being with no memory, with no family…"

I stared at her scar.

"Enough!" I barked.

"But, Daniel, we must talk about it…"

"All right, let's talk about it!"

"The most wonderful part," she went on, "is that I'm a complete being, educated… Relatively so, of course. What I mean is I know what everybody knows… And then there is the fact that this being is brand new! I'm Mademoiselle No-name! And I come from No-where. I was born three weeks ago on the

Barcelona road. You, and you alone, are my creator, my father, my mother, my brother, my lover…"

"You think about all that?"

"Of course. You don't think I lie around for hours on the beach like a pebble?"

So she thought about all that… Still, she didn't think she might be Madame No-name, rather than Mademoiselle. Nor did she pause to think that she had a child…

"And I'd like to say another thing, Daniel…"

"What?"

"I have no wish to know who I am. I have no wish to know anyone else but you. The past doesn't bother me. What matters is the present. And of course the future too!…"

I hugged her close to me. I choked on my tears.

"Thank you, Marianne, for being here and for loving me so much. All right, we'll leave your past where it is…"

There was a silence. We were both thinking about the same problem: identity documents, the damned proof of pedigree which men require of each other. The numbers and labels they hang around their necks so they can be pigeonholed and regimented.

"Listen, Marianne, I've got an idea!"

"Yes?"

"I'll get you a set of false papers… It should be possible, don't you think? Gangsters get hold of them, no sweat. All I do is pay whatever it costs and they're in the bag."

"You really think so?"

"Yes, only I don't think we can do it here. I can't speak Spanish and I'd be swindled. I'll fly to Paris and sort it out when I'm there…"

"You'll be leaving me here?"

"Only for a few days, just long enough to do the necessary."

She let it go at that. She knew very well that it was the only solution if we were to call time on her ambiguous situation.

"I can't think of any other way… I'll take some photos of you which will have to be attached to the official documents…"

"And after that?"

"After that… Wait a second… The big problem, once I've got the passport, will be how to have it stamped with an entry visa into Spain so that we can get it stamped again when we leave…"

And then I burst out laughing.

"How stupid can I be? It's not a problem! To cross a border, you go to the customs post to have the passports stamped while your car is being checked by the border guards. I'll just get both of them stamped instead of one, as if you were travelling with me. But that means I'll have to take the car, because otherwise it won't work… It's crazy, because my return trip will take at least three days longer, but it's worth it."

"Whatever you say…"

I kissed her. I was pleased with my brainwave… Yes, thanks to my little scheme, I'd have a ghost for a travelling companion, someone who owed her existence to me.

"Come on, let's make the most of the remaining light to take those photos of you."

We climbed out through the small window. That way we avoided having to go out through the Casa. Outside, behind the building, was a kind of small terrace which caught the last of the day's sun. I set the shutter speed according to the directions I'd been given in the shop to take close-ups of Marianne.

I used up the whole roll of film to take her from different angles. I'd select the best of them.

"I'll leave as soon as they're developed!" I said as I put the camera back in its case.

"Then I hope they never are!"

"Come on, darling, you know it has to be done. But we won't be apart for long, I promise... One week!"

And what will I do all that time?"

Wait for me here. You've got a routine now, your own room, the beach, they know you here!"

"All right."

The idea of having to leave her was torture. I kept asking myself too: "And what if she isn't here when you get back?"

But I pushed the thought away with all my strength. Nothing could come between us. I'd go all the way!

She went to her room to put a skirt on. I'd bought her a lot of clothes in bright colours. They suited her very well. When we walked around Barcelona, all the men gave her the eye. The average Spaniard, so reserved with the women of his own country, is rather more than flirtatious when it comes to women from abroad.

When she came back, I was lying on my bed, with my hands behind my head, staring at a hairline crack in the ceiling.

"What's that there?" she murmured. I looked. She'd just noticed the violin case which was propped up against my easel.

It was a really big moment for me. I held my breath, the way you would if you came across a sleepwalker in a dangerous place and were afraid to wake them.

Marianne bent down and picked up the black case. Its round shoulders gleamed dully in the semi-darkness.

She opened it and with one finger gently plucked the strings.

I kept my eyes half closed so that I wouldn't distract her. She took the instrument out, then freed the bow... Judging by the way she cradled the violin under her chin, I knew that she was an experienced player. It was a clean, practised movement. She tested the strings with the bow and adjusted the tuning pegs... For a moment she composed herself, then suddenly, with disconcerting directness, she launched into Tchaikovsky's Violin Concerto in D minor. As she played, I was overcome by a feeling I hadn't known before that moment. It was something between admiration and regret, something I couldn't get in focus.

She played with consummate artistry, her head inclined to one side, her eyes half closed, her hair tumbling down on each side of the violin.

I spent unforgettable minutes listening to her. I was paralysed by my feelings. The puffy face of Tejero appeared behind the glass of the window. His eyes were filled with pious respect.

When she'd finished what she was playing, and before I could say a word, she went straight into a Mozart serenade, *Eine kleine Nachtmusik* I think it was, and it was as if heaven itself was being poured into my ears.

It didn't seem possible to me that such music should stir no memory in her poor, amnesic brain... Since she was playing scores by heart, she must be seeing the notes on a page in front of her. There was therefore no reason why she shouldn't also rediscover, with more or less clarity, the ambiance of the place where she'd learnt them and the shadowy figure of the teacher who'd taught them to her.

She stopped suddenly in the middle of a bar.

"Go on!" I begged her.

She shook her head sadly.

"I can't remember any more."

"But you've had no problem playing this far…"

"I played without thinking about it… and then suddenly everything went black… It all got hazy…"

As she spoke, she put the violin back into its case.

"Is it yours, Daniel?"

"No, it's yours. I just bought it for you in Barcelona."

"That's amazing! How could you know that I played?"

I hesitated.

"Listen, Marianne, when I knocked you over with my car, you had a violin case under your arm."

"I did?"

"Yes… The instrument was smashed to smithereens in the collision… So I bought you another as a present so that…"

"You thought that it would unlock something in my head?"

"I… yes, I think that was what I had in mind."

She sat down by the black case and stroked it with the tips of her fingers. She was thinking.

"Actually," she murmured, "it did conjure up an image."

I passed a hand over my eyes. I was afraid, but also hungry to know. When she didn't say any more, I snapped:

"Go on, then, what was it?"

"What was what, Daniel?"

"Whatever you saw… The image!"

She put up one hand in front of her eyes, like a screen.

"I see a window… with embroidered curtains… The hasp of the window is in the form of a lion's head with its jaws wide open… Outside the window is the thick branch of a tree which sways gently…"

"What else?"

I had grabbed her by the wrist and was shaking her. When I released her, her hand was very white. I took it and raised it to my lips.

"Tell me, Marianne, what else do you see?"

"That's it."

"How do you mean? All the music reminds you of is a window?"

"Yes. Because I was playing in front of it."

"Try again!"

"No, it's no good, I tell you, my head is full of cement... Besides, I told you, I don't want to remember."

Tejero's face had vanished from the window frame.

We set off towards the village to get the roll of film developed.

# 11

The photographs came out well and I set off two days later at night. Since the usual goodbyes would have been too painful for both of us, I left just as the Casa Patricio was settling down for the night.

I'd written a letter for her which I'd left with old Señora Patricio to give to her, together with enough money to cover our hotel expenses. In the letter I added a few suggestions about what she might do at the Casa during my absence, and naturally I included the kind of crazy things people write in their own blood when they're in love.

My car was now parked in the road, for I'd moved it there after taking one last swim while Marianne was getting changed in her room. So, on the stroke of two, I climbed out of my window and got to my car.

As I opened the door, my heart almost stopped. Marianne was there, in the front seat. Her eyes gleamed strangely in the dark.

She smiled at me.

"I knew you were leaving tonight, Daniel…"

"How did you know?"

"There's nothing mysterious how about it. I saw you getting the car out earlier this evening… I realized you were intending to go without saying anything, to spare us the tears… You were probably right…But I'm not going to cry… I just wanted to tell you something before we separated…"

I got into the car. I'd already become used to having her at my side when I drove. I put one hand on her shoulder.

"What is it you wanted to tell me, my darling?"

"Daniel, the other day the violin made me remember that music, didn't it?"

"Yes. So?"

"So you better know that… being loved by you hasn't made me remember anything. I'm absolutely certain I've never loved other men, Daniel, never! Yes, you had to know. I may have met other men, but I never loved any of them, it's unthinkable… Do you understand?"

I laid my head on her breast and I was the one weeping in the dark.

That she should admit such a thing took my breath away.

She held my head in both hands and made me straighten up. Gently, she kissed my eyes. Then she murmured:

"Now go!"

And then she was no longer there. I wanted to call after her, but I stopped myself. I was ashamed of my weakness.

I saw her graceful silhouette emerge from the shadow of the pine wood and skip over the moon-splashed sand. Then she vanished behind the Casa Patricio and I was left infinitely alone in my car with the murmur of the sea and the dancing fireflies.

I shook myself and turned the key in the starter. Force of habit has a calming influence that soothes our woes.

The wheels of the car skidded on the sand. I got out and put a pine branch under them. I managed to drive the car out of the loose earth and then, as usual, pitched and lurched my way to the deserted main road where, on a night just like this, it had all started for us.

# PART THREE

# 12

The greater the distance between Marianne and me became, the more aware I was of her predicament. Until then, I'd been interested in her only as a person of flesh and blood and, not without a degree of cowardice, I'd banished her past from my preoccupations. But now, alone in my car and freed from her spell, I began to think seriously.

I'd managed to overlook one crucial fact which coloured the whole incident: she'd thrown herself at my car. To reach the point of carrying out such a desperate act she must have been through hell. Maybe she'd come to Spain with a man and maybe the man had left her?

If I wanted to keep her I'd have to settle her in some out-of-the-way spot like Castelldefels... in a place where no one from her past life was likely to appear out of the blue and wave to her and shout her name. That was what scared me. She was now so completely mine that I couldn't have borne it if anyone else became close to her and talked to her about people or things I'd never heard of.

If she were to have complete freedom of movement, I needed to obtain papers for her. Of course, that was why I'd come to France, but now that I was driving along our own roads, my scheme stopped being theoretical and became a pressing problem I had to solve. I wasn't at all sure how to set about these things. I had half an idea that there were people in Pigalle and such places who specialized in forging documents, but I didn't know who they were and I couldn't think of anyone I knew who might be able to point me in their direction. It was then that

I had the idea that I might break the law myself. It would be safer and it wouldn't cost as much. But where would I start?

I was driving without really concentrating, simply following my habit of being behind the wheel. The kilometres tripped along on the dial of my speedometer and I didn't feel at all tired. I snatched a quick lunch at Toulouse and stopped at Limoges, intending to spend the night there. But after I'd had dinner I felt refreshed and continued my mad dash to Paris.

Driving is a kind of drug. When I drive for long periods I'm overtaken by a kind of torpor. My subconscious takes over the wheel. It's my subconscious that dips the headlights and registers the illuminated garlands that signal the presence of parked lorries ahead of me. It's my subconscious that slams on the brakes...

At such times, I think with unusual clarity. My sharply tuned nerves become the eager servants of my brain.

It is as if I have an erupting volcano inside me.

I sorted out the problem of the documents between Limoges and Orléans. Basically, it was quite simple. My mother was still alive. For the last eight years she'd been living in a nursing home after being almost completely immobilized by paralysis. All I had to do was to send a postal application in her name to the town hall of the place where she was born and request a copy of her birth certificate, the date of which I would alter. It would require some fine, close work, but when I was an adolescent I was particularly adept at falsifying my school reports. My skill was such that even my friends would ask me to use my small talent on their behalf, so they could avoid unpleasant interviews with their fathers.

Once that was done I'd go to my local police station to obtain a certificate of residence by submitting the birth certificate made out in my mother's name as proof of identity, along with a rent book also with her name on it… They'd let me have the document without a second glance. All I would need to do then was fill out a passport application, submitting the birth certificate and the proof of address together with the photos of Marianne. I wouldn't go to the prefecture in person for that might arouse suspicion. Instead I'd do it through Touring-Club, the motoring organization of which I was a member… In four or five days I'd have the documents. I'd use them to ask for a new Spanish visa for myself. Since both passports had the same name on them, it'd go through on the nod. It was summer, and at passport control the staff would be pretty busy.

With a bit of luck, I'd get the visa date-stamped on my way back into Spain and then we'd have no problems leaving the country. What I liked about this plan was that it didn't implicate Marianne in any way. If it backfired, I'd be the one in the soup, and anyway no one would send me to the guillotine for forging a few documents.

When I got to Orléans, I felt that if I didn't stop I'd wrap myself around a pylon. A town clock was striking two. I spotted a couple of constables doing their night rounds and asked them if they could direct me to a hotel. Ten minutes later I was flopping down on a creaky bed, feeling that I'd never be able to get up again.

## 13

What took longest was waiting for my mother's birth certificate
to be sent back to me. My mother was born at Saint-Omer and
I had to wait three long days for my letter to the chief clerk at
the town hall to get there and for the certificate to reach me.

To kill the time spent waiting and to relax a little, I called
on a few painter friends, but the sun had emptied their stu-
dios and I found nothing but locked doors everywhere. I had
to resort to Brutin, the director of the gallery. He greeted me
as if I'd won the Tour de France. He took me to dinner and,
over dessert, handed me a cheque which was a very welcome
addition to my bank account.

He asked me about Spain, whether I was painting, about
life there... I gave him monosyllabic answers.

"You don't seem to be in particularly good shape, Mermet.
Health problems?"

"No..."

"You look as if you've lost weight."

"It's Spanish cooking, I can't get used to it."

"Are you sure you haven't fallen in love?"

Brutin was a fat man, as bald as an egg, who wore square,
rimless glasses and thought that wearing a dark suit made him
look serious, although his entire being was already a hymn to
gravitas.

"Be careful, we don't want any foul-ups just now! You're
on the up! Your name is getting to be known and you have
no idea how fast fame spreads! You'll be getting all sorts of
invitations..."

"I prefer cheques, Monsieur Brutin."

"Come off it! No artist talks like that!"

"The myth about the starving artist is dying out. I think people have finally realized that the man of genius has a belly that needs filling, that well-cut clothes suit him as well as other men, that he can occasionally drive a car and doesn't have to live in squalor to produce beautiful things!"

That amused him. He began to laugh.

"I like you. I don't regret backing you. Up to now, I've not seen much of a return on you but I have a feeling that the wind is about to change. I'll make all the arrangements for your American campaign for you!"

"I don't much fancy going to the United States just now, Monsieur Brutin."

That rocked him. He removed his square glasses. Without them, he looked like an exotic fish.

"What did you say?"

"I said I don't want to go to America for the moment. I'm working well, I feel that I'm in full control of my talent and I wouldn't want to run the risk of choking off this surge of creativity by going on a publicity tour."

He nodded.

"Yes, I can understand that… Anyway, we'll talk about it another time. Are you staying in Paris?"

"No, I'm going back to Spain."

"When?"

"This week."

"Good God! So why did you come back?"

"Money!"

"You should have phoned me. I've got an agent in Barcelona. He would have advanced you whatever you needed."

"Ah yes, that's a pity. Never mind, I'm here now…"

So the evening was cut short. I was as miserable as hell. I pictured Marianne all alone in her room in the Casa Patricio. The sun still cast lingering trails over the sea. The lights of the fishing boats were beginning to show. I knew that she'd be crying. I could sense it. She was feeling the same heartache as I was. It gnawed at her like some secret hurt. No one could do anything for her except me, and no one else could do anything for me. We were one single being temporarily split into two.

I left Brutin, saying that I was exhausted after my journey.

But I didn't feel ready for bed. It was one of those warm, dusty evenings such as you get only in Paris in the summer. The sky was almost white and it seemed that the daylight would never fade.

I decided to go for a spin in the car before going back to my studio in the Rue Falguière.

I drove up the Champs-Elysées as far as the Bois de Boulogne, which I crossed diagonally and came out at the Seine near Saint-Cloud. Couples embraced under the full-leafed trees and cars proceeded slowly along the access roads. The whole of the Bois was full of the scent of summer and love. I felt that the entire green space was in the grip of something overpoweringly strong. Other people's love filled me with disgust. Only mine was real…

As long as I would really be reunited with *her* at the Casa Patricio. As long as in my absence the Spanish police hadn't dug up something about her… As long as they hadn't sent for her to attend for interview… I'd thought of everything, except that… I'd left her countless instructions except one covering a summons to appear for official interview. What would she do alone in Barcelona? I was afraid she'd come to grief, that some new shock…

A cool breeze told me I was nearing the Seine. I emerged onto the esplanade at Longchamp, and through the trees I caught sight of a white boat crowded with people reclining in deckchairs. I stopped for a while to enjoy the peace of the evening. At Castelldefels everything was too garish, too loud: the dawns, the twilights, the torrid days… There I felt it was like living in a painting by Van Gogh, whereas this corner of Paris encapsulated the sweetness of living.

At that moment I needed her, needed to show her this because she'd forgotten such things.

I restarted the car, taking my time. Prostitutes in summer dresses gave me cautious glances. I followed the river as far as the bridge at Saint-Cloud and suddenly a road sign caught my eye: *Western Motorway. Versailles–Saint-Germain*!

It wasn't far to the town where Marianne had bought her clothes and where perhaps… I turned right, crossed the bridge, navigated the roundabout and then took the slip road leading to the motorway tunnel.

She was waiting for me… Not only at Castelldefels but here in Saint-Germain. There was a lingering trace of her under the skies of the Île-de-France and it was calling to me.

Once I got to the motorway I picked up my speed. I passed the first turn-off to Vaucresson then took the second which led me past the old SHAPE base.

A quarter of an hour later I was at Saint-Germain.

The small town was full of the smell of faded lilac. A drowsy hush was settling over the place. All the windows gaped. A few cafés were still open. I stopped when I got to the Place du

Chasseur. I parked my car in front of the small railway station and sat down at a table on a terrace.

There were the sounds of children and booming radios, and yet the evening remained untroubled and fragile with its stubborn smell of endangered vegetation and the cool air that blew in from the forest.

The white-jacketed waiter who served me was old and riddled with rheumatism. He must have been there ever since the café had opened long ago and had grown decrepit with it.

"Yes, sir?"

I wasn't thirsty… My eye happened to fall on the sign with "ICES" written on it in fancy lettering.

"I'll have an ice cream."

"Strawberry? Vanilla? Mocha?"

This passion for ice cream was a leftover from my childhood. And just as I used to, and with the same secret gluttony behind my words, I murmured:

"Strawberry!"

When he came back with the metal dish capped with a pinkish dome, I was holding a photograph of Marianne in my hand.

"Tell me, waiter…"

"Sir?"

"Have you lived in Saint-Germain for long?"

"I was born here, sir…"

"I'd like to ask you something…"

"I'd be delighted to help you if I can, sir."

I held out the photo.

It showed Marianne in a bathing costume with her eyes half closed against the sun. Visible on the extreme left of the picture was the bamboo lean-to of the Casa Patricio.

The old man didn't understand.

"Just look at the person in the photo and tell me if you ever saw her before."

But it was me he looked at, making no attempt to hide his surprise. Then he realized that I was just an ordinary sort of man. He started feeling in the inside pocket of his white jacket. He produced a pair of old spectacles which he perched on the end of his nose. Only then did he look at the photo.

My fingers were as cold as ice. I tried to read the expression on his face but all I saw was a look of intense concentration.

Then he raised his eyes thoughtfully. "I couldn't really say, sir… I see so many faces…"

"Ring any bells?"

"I have a feeling that this face is vaguely familiar… Does this person live in Saint-Germain?"

"She did for a while…"

He shook his head and put his specs away.

"She's young and pretty. You must remember that Saint-Germain is a student town… I see many of them, a great many, you wouldn't believe the half of it… To be honest, sir, I couldn't swear to anything…"

"But at least you feel that you might have seen her before?"

"Unless I'm mixing her up…"

It wasn't much but it was encouraging. I say encouraging, because ever since I'd set foot in this town, I'd been filled with a burning need to know.

"Thank you, sorry to have…"

But he didn't move. I had roused his curiosity and he wanted to know too. Actually I felt I owed him an explanation.

"This is a young woman my brother used to know. I don't know her name. The only thing I do know about her is that she used to live in Saint-Germain or hereabouts. My brother is abroad, in the colonies…"

And I then embarked on a fanciful tale which he swallowed without batting an eyelid.

"Do you have any ideas I could follow up?" I asked. "I can hardly walk around town stopping everyone I meet and showing them the photo, can I?"

He gave it some thought. I was the only customer left on the terrace. The *patron*, who wore a waistcoat, stood yawning behind his till. They were waiting for me to leave before they could close.

"You should go and see the parish priest… the doctors… You know, people who deal with everybody in a town."

"Yes, that's not a bad idea."

My ice cream had melted. I gave the old man a large tip and went back to my car.

# 14

At eight the next morning I was back in Saint-Germain.

I found the presbytery, rang the bell at the gate and asked to see the *curé*. I had to wait for some time because he was saying mass, but I wasn't put out at having to kick my heels because it gave me time to put the finishing touches to a plausible story—and even more so because the room where the serving girl had told me to wait was wonderfully conducive to reflection. There was a strong smell of floor polish, all the austere furniture was dark and a huge crucifix filled an entire section of the back wall. I told myself that when I spoke to the priest it would be best to get straight to the point. So when he came in—a tall, attentive figure, with wide myopic eyes and unhurried gestures—I didn't give him time to ask questions.

"I'm sorry to bother you, Canon (I'd noticed the red border of his cassock). I'm with the crime squad."

With a very professional gesture, I fingered my lapel, though without going so far as to turn it back.

Without further ado I put the photograph of Marianne down on his desk.

"I'm attached to Missing Persons, Family division. I'm currently making enquiries about a young woman. A case of amnesia. That's her picture. Her clothes have the label of a dressmaker based in this area, which leads me to think that she might be from Saint-Germain too."

He looked at the photograph and shook his head.

"I don't know this person, inspector."

"Are you quite sure, Canon?"

"Perfectly."

He gave the picture back to me.

"Couldn't they help you in the shop?"

"What shop?"

"Why... the shop you mentioned, the one that sold her the garments?"

I hadn't thought of that. The priest saw that I hadn't and couldn't suppress a smile. I must have given him a low opinion of the police!

I clearly remembered the name of the shop: it was Février, not an easy one to forget. It was located in the main street, not far from the post office. It was a very modern shop and went back a long way. As I walked through the door I felt a pang because I was certain that Marianne had been here at some point in her past.

A shop assistant came up to me. She was a helpful, bright girl. I went through the routine about being a policeman because basically it was the simplest explanation and the most effective. People always try to satisfy the curiosity of the police. It's human nature.

She listened to me without saying anything, but her small eyes, like a blackbird's, sparkled with excitement.

When I held out the photo for her after running through my story, she put out one hand. It was trembling. This time there was no hesitation.

"Yes, I recognize the lady."

"Does she live at Saint-Germain?"

"I imagine so. I've met her several times. When she came to buy a blouse I was the one who served her. She had her baby with her."

The effect on me was the equivalent of having a bucket of water thrown in my face. Her baby! So I hadn't been mistaken.

"How old was the child?"

"Perhaps two?... He played in the shop..."

She gave me a look of surprise. She couldn't understand why I'd gone as white as a sheet. Especially since policemen are supposed to keep cool in all circumstances.

"Er... you..."

"What?"

"You wouldn't have any idea of exactly where she might live?"

"No. But I don't think she lives in the centre of Saint-Germain because I didn't see her very often..."

That was all, but it was plenty.

I left, rather unsteady on my feet, and went for a strong drink in the nearby bistro.

With her baby!

The words were like a dagger in my heart. Her baby! So it was true!

I wanted to get out of there, to abandon my quest... But I stayed.

## 15

I walked through the sunny streets of the little town. It was market day, and braying crowds ebbed and flowed along the narrow thoroughfares. I allowed myself to be jostled without complaining by housewives laden with baskets. I felt slightly queasy. I was thinking that Marianne had lived in this town. The notion that another man had held her in his arms, that he was the father of her child…

She'd seemed so distant, so far away, in the white-painted Casa and on the wide beach lit by an infernal sun. I saw her, so to speak, through the wrong end of a telescope. She was tiny, out of my reach. There was a whole world between us. I'd just crossed the frontier to the land of her past and it was just as if I was now watching her from a point inside her old life.

My eagerness to know more grew stronger and stronger… I needed to see the house she'd lived in… To see her son, her husband… To breathe the musty fragrance of her "yesterdays".

Then I stopped. The answer was there, at my fingertips. All I had to do was think. I knew that she lived in Saint-Germain or its suburbs. I knew that she had a child and that it hadn't been an easy birth. Therefore she must have had the baby in a clinic in the area, or in hospital.

At that moment I happened to be walking past a cul-de-sac flanked by two very large red crosses on a white background.

A sign said: *Hospital. Quiet, please!*

I turned into it and started walking between two long walls. I passed through a gate then proceeded over the fine gravel of a well-raked path.

Inside the hospital building I looked for directions. An arrow pointed me to the gynaecology department. It was filled with bawling babies. Recently arrived citizens were asserting their unshakeable will to live.

I went inside. The place was filled with the stale smell of sour milk and ether. Ward assistants came and went with armfuls of dirty linen. Others pushed trolleys laden with food that looked pretty tasteless.

I stood in the midst of all this hustle and bustle like a straw-chewing yokel marooned at a Paris crossroads. A fat nurse with chubby cheeks and a moustache barked at me:

"It's not visiting hours. Are you a new father?"

I got a grip on myself.

"Police!"

That took some of the wind out of her sails.

I repeated my story. I knew it now by heart, which allowed me to play the part with more authority.

She was curious. During her long night watches she probably lapped up the latest issues of women's magazines and had read every word Georges Ohnet ever wrote.

"Have you ever seen this person?"

She gave a cry:

"I certainly have… It's the Renard girl…"

"You're sure?"

"Absolutely! She stayed here for a month… I assisted the doctor who delivered her, because I should tell you…"

"I know!"

I couldn't bear to hear the details. I found it all odious.

"Did you say Renard?"

"Yes."

"Marianne Renard?"

"Yes, I believe that was her name."

"Do you know where her husband lives?"

She gave a shrug.

"Didn't have one."

Decidedly, it was one surprise after the other… No husband! Marianne was an unmarried mother. It hardly corresponded to the impression she gave…

"Did she have a family?"

"No, nobody… her mother had just died…"

"Where did she live?"

"I don't know… But they'll be able to tell you in the bursar's office. Ask them to look in the admissions register. It was… wait a minute… two years ago last February…"

"Thank you."

However, everything almost went wrong for me at the bursar's office… There I spoke to a pettifogging little martinet with a red moustache who asked me to prove I was a policeman. I had the presence of mind to back down and admit that I was a private detective and that I was acting on behalf of our client. He showed me the door and I found myself standing on the edge of a lawn watching a gardener watering with a hosepipe, not knowing what had hit me. I felt humiliated, because it is always humiliating to get kicked out of anywhere.

Especially because there had been a very good-looking secretary in the office. As I was on my way out, she ran after me. She wasn't very tall, had dark hair, green eyes and an adorable smile. She had thrown a jacket over her shoulders.

"You mustn't mind the bursar, he's got a weak liver," she said. "While you were talking to him, I looked for the information you wanted. The person you were asking about lives at 14 Rue des Gros-Murs."

"You're an angel!"

She was probably expecting me to ask her for a date, because it was my good looks alone that had made her so helpful. But I didn't have the heart for it…

I left her after flashing her a comforting smile. I was anxious to find the Rue des Gros-Murs.

# 16

The house looked sad and romantic. It was an old building which hid its crumbling façade behind trees which no one had remembered to prune.

A rusty double gate overhung with clusters of mauve wisteria barred the entrance to the garden. All the shutters were closed.

I leant with my back against the wall of the house opposite and stared for some time at the empty house.

"So," I said to myself, "is this where she lived?"

There was something mysterious, even disturbing about the place. I couldn't take my eyes off it.

After a while I heard a faint rustle quite near to me. I turned and saw an old woman in the window of a neighbouring house. She was looking at me with the avid curiosity which citizens in the provinces always evince when they come across anything unusual. She smiled.

"There's no one there," she said.

I moved nearer to her. She was a very old lady. She had only one tooth left in the middle of her mouth which made her look like a cartoon figure out of the pages of *L'Assiette au beurre*.

"Are you're looking for Mademoiselle Renard?"

"As a matter of fact... yes."

"She's gone away. Been gone nearly a month..."

"You... you wouldn't happen to know where she is?"

"Oh yes," the old girl said coolly. "She's in Spain."

It rocked me to the core.

She caught my reaction, which seemed to put new life in her.

"You better come in," she said.

I opened her gate. She came to greet me at her front door.

"Are you a friend of hers?"

"No… I… I'm from Social Security and I've come to enquire about her baby…"

"Oh…"

She seemed rather disappointed.

"Did she go to Spain by herself?"

"No, she went with her little boy and her old gentleman."

I winced visibly.

"What old gentleman?"

It made the old girl's day. She licked her moustache for the taste of it.

"You know… Bridon… Old man Bridon! You've never heard of him? Bridon's jam? It's the son now who's taken the business over…"

She had the whole story by heart and it gave her inordinate pleasure to roll it out once more for a new audience.

"You're not from around here?"

"No, from Paris…"

"Ah, that explains it… Well, let me tell you the full story…"

By all means tell me! I wanted to know. I had to plumb the depths of the abyss. I knew now that I wouldn't much like what I was about to find there.

Perhaps the most painful part of it was to hear it from the lips of an old crone for whom Marianne's story was just another excuse for malicious gossip.

"She lost her father when she was quite young… He worked in the registry office in town. A very respectable family, you can take it from me…"

I was seething with impatience but I had to submit. She didn't do things by halves. With her it was all or nothing.

"When her father died Marianne was still a little girl. Her mother ran through the money… Drink," she sighed… "She'd spend all day drinking while all the time pretending she was ever so ladylike. But that didn't stop her being what you might call dead to the world every night and that poor kid was left to do everything around the house…"

I had anticipated a sorry tale of this sort ever since I saw the desolate look in Marianne's eyes. The odd thing was that the longer the toothless neighbour droned on, the more I felt I was hearing a story I already knew. I thought of my portrait of Marianne which was in the boot of the car and I knew that the glint in her eye there said it all.

"She had a gentleman friend, old Bridon… a real swine, that man… Depraved and worse! There were terrible scenes in front of young Marianne when the mother had been drinking… Of course, Madame Renard didn't love him, but he gave them just enough money for them to get by… One night she had an attack of… wait a minute, I can't remember what they call it…"

I muttered:

"Alcohol poisoning."

That sent me up in the neighbour's estimation.

"Yes, that's it… Albertine—that's Marianne's mother— threw herself out of a window. That one, there…"

With one finger twisted with rheumatism, she pointed to a window on the house opposite.

"They found her next morning lying on the pavement… She was still alive but she died in hospital… Old Bridon continued to come, and now the girl became his mistress. Believe it if you want, but that miserable old… so-and-so… fathered a child on

92

her! At his age! Marianne hardly went out any more except to the shops, which was where I used to meet her. And even then he used to play hell with her if he happened to come and she wasn't there… He used to hit her… I used to hear the screams and every time I felt like reporting him to the police… But you know how it is, don't you? In small towns like this, afterwards nobody thanks you for it… All poor Marianne had was her violin… She was always playing it… I don't think she looked after the baby… Which means to say that it wasn't much more than a little animal that never set foot outside the door…"

"Here, are you crying?" she said.

"There's every reason to, isn't there?"

"Yes… When I used to see Marianne and talk to her about her old man, she'd tell me every time that he was going to take her to Spain. It's all she ever thought about… it was getting to be an obsession…"

I broke in:

"Did you ever have a feeling that she… that she wasn't altogether normal?"

"How do you mean?"

I gave my answer by tapping my temple.

"Oh, like that…"

She thought about the question as if it was the first time that anyone had asked her.

"No, though perhaps she wasn't quite all there. She looked so sad, it was pitiful to see her," she sighed. "She spoke in a monotonous sort of voice, without moving a muscle in her face. It used to break my heart…"

"What happened then?"

"A month ago, one morning, the milkman… because here, since we're a bit out of the way, the milkman delivers to the door… Anyway, he was doing his round. She told him she wouldn't be wanting any more milk because she was going to Spain. I asked her, by way of conversation, if she was going by herself, and she said no, that she was going with Bridon and the child…"

"And then?"

"I never saw her after that… When I woke up the next day, the place was all locked up."

So now I knew. The truth was even more tragic than I could have imagined. It was the most heartbreaking, the most disquieting story I'd ever heard. And it was the story of the woman I loved.

I felt tired. I was suddenly aware of how weary I was. Tired of begging for scraps of Marianne's past from complete strangers…

"You're not going already?"

"I have to."

I stopped for another moment by the rusted gate. A strange silence hung over the untended garden… I pressed myself against the metal bars of the gate. I felt it move. I glanced up at the old woman's house. She wasn't at her window. She'd seen me to her door and because she dragged herself about rather than walked, she hadn't had time to return to her observation post. I raised the latch of the iron gate and walked into the grounds.

# 17

Inside hung a scent of death, or more accurately, a cemetery smell, though it comes to the same thing. Yes, it was exactly the same clinging, pervasive, depressing smell of places like that. An odour floating on a base of rotting vegetation. Grass and brambles covered the whole of the garden. The choked shoots of irises were dying under the rubble which had fallen from a crumbling wall. A broken swing hung by a single chain from the low branch of an apple tree.

I advanced slowly over what I could make out of the garden path towards the moss-grown steps up to the front door. This time I felt I was physically entering Marianne's past. Here was her memory and I was padding quietly through it…

I climbed the steps. There was a double door with glass in the upper halves. Behind the glass was a wrought-iron screen. I held out one hand and touched the glass next to the latch. I couldn't say what secret impulse urged me on. I felt the pane loose under my fingers. The putty had fallen out and the small tacks which held it in had rusted through.

All I had to do was to push a little harder for the whole pane to give way. It didn't fall, for it was held by the wrought ironwork. I managed to slide half of my hand inside, far enough to enable me to reach the knob on the lock. After several attempts I succeeded in turning it. The door opened by itself.

I stepped into a mouldering passageway sweating with damp. So was this the depressing background to her submerged life?

It was enough to make you want to scream. It was like a simplified version of Sartre's *No Exit*, but rather more tragically banal.

I pushed the door. It opened onto a sitting room. But what a sitting room! The wallpaper hung down in frayed strips. What remained stuck to the walls was blistered and stained. I stood facing the window. In front of it was a music stand. On it was a Tchaikovsky score: it was open. I also noticed that the hasp of the window was in the form of a lion with gaping jaws.

It was here in this room that Marianne had played... I knew that if I opened the shutters I'd see the branch of a tree just outside the window pane... But I refrained from doing so because of the old woman, who'd be back at her post by now.

The door opposite led to a dining room furnished in rococo style. I didn't even go in. What I wanted to see was another even more hellish room: the bedroom! The four walls where the unspeakable fornications of the old satyr had taken place.

Once I'd done that, I knew I'd be over the worst of the shock, make my way back to the Casa Patricio and face her, buoyed up not only by my love but also by a pity that knew no bounds.

Creaking stairs led upwards at the end of the passageway. I began climbing them. As I neared the top, I felt my nose and the back of my throat tighten in the grip of an appalling stench, the source of which I couldn't locate. I concluded that as she left, Marianne had forgotten some perishable items somewhere.

On the first-floor landing, two further doors invited my attention. I opened one and knew immediately that it led not to a bedroom but hell itself!

Two slats were missing from the latticed shutters and the room glowed as if in the light of an aquarium. A body lay on the bed. It was the body of an old man. Putrefaction had begun its foul work… The sheets under it were reddish brown. I realized it was the blood that he'd lost and which had subsequently dried. The neck had been brutally slashed, as had the lower abdomen. She'd attacked him with demented savagery. On the bedside rug lay an antique dagger. The blade had been bent. It was what she'd used to kill him.

# 18

The small number of people who've unexpectedly come across a dead body and claim that they felt afraid, are lying. I know that I experienced a multitude of very different reactions when I found Bridon's carcass, but fear didn't figure among them. What I was aware of was, above all, an indescribable sense of stupor and a distinct feeling of nausea. And with good cause… The pestilential presence of the corpse was so overpowering that I took a few steps back and threw up. I don't think there can be a sight more repulsive than that dead body with its swollen belly and mangled, greenish flesh.

As I stumbled backwards, I caught sight of a cot behind the door. More of a small bed, really, but with a large white muslin veil draped over it… I couldn't say why I lifted the veil. There are circumstances in which we respond to uncontrollable reflexes. I know now that I shall never forget the sight of that small dead infant. There wasn't a mark on the body. It had starved to death.

For a moment I closed my eyes. I couldn't believe what I was seeing. The reality of it was too great for any man. It caused my entire nervous system to shut down, the way an electric surge will cause a weak fuse to blow.

I staggered out of there, slamming the bedroom door behind me. I couldn't stand it any longer. I was utterly unable to take any more. It was like something out of Dante.

Clutching the banister, I went down the stairs. When I got to the bottom, I sat down on the last step. My head was spinning. The stench from the room made me feel as if I'd been drinking. It had entered into me and I thought I'd never be rid of it. The words of the doctor in Barcelona came back to me: "It's not certain that it was the trauma that brought on her condition... No, she may have already lost her memory before it happened."

The horror of it all made me shake, but far from laying the blame for it on Marianne, I felt, on the contrary, increasingly sorry for her. The poor creature, kept locked up and violated, was entitled to claim all manner of extenuating circumstances. Little by little she'd lost her reason—no, not exactly her reason, but all sense of reality. She'd allowed her baby to become anaemic and then had just stopped taking care of it. The child had died... One day, after old Bridon had satisfied his lust with her, she'd had a fit of uncontrollable range and murdered him. And then she'd picked up her violin...

Spain!

Hadn't the first words she'd spoken at Castelldefels been something like: "I always dreamt of going to Spain"?

Why Spain? Because of the sun, the light... In this house full of darkness and icy draughts, she'd already been dreaming of the Casa Patricio even before she'd seen it. She'd sensed it. And she'd surely also dreamt of a man like me, young and strong, who'd hold her to his manly chest... who'd wash her clean of the obscene caresses of that old man...

Yes, in me she found the lover she'd always been waiting for. But how the devil had she managed to get herself all the way to Barcelona? It was a mystery to which the key would never be found...

I stood up. The two bodies upstairs had, in life, been unbearable presences for her. Father and son... How she must have hated the child who was an extension of the immortal Bridon! Even Zola never dreamt up a story more sordid than this.

I walked as far as the front steps. The cemetery smell was now explained. As I closed the door, the garden gate creaked. I turned quickly. A beefy man in a beige raincoat had just come in. You didn't have to be very smart to see that he, at least, was a policeman—a real one.

# 19

The scent of danger snapped me out of my daze. I assumed a casual air.

"Who are you?" he asked.

He didn't say it: he barked.

"I'm a Social Security inspector…"

I gestured to the house.

"You can walk into this place like it's liberty hall… but there's no one at home."

"Are you sure?"

"I've just had a look round."

I pretended to be frank and open.

"Do you live here?" I asked.

"No. I'm from the Saint-Germain police. I'm making enquiries about a missing person…"

My blood turned colder than spring water.

"Someone local?"

"Yes… Name of Bridon… His son hasn't seen him for a month."

"You don't say. Maybe he's gone travelling somewhere?"

"Can't be. He hasn't withdrawn any money from his bank account…"

Then, realizing he was revealing professional secrets to an ordinary member of the public, he gave a shrug.

"We'll find him…"

He passed in front of me and started up the steps. I heard bells ringing in my ears and red sparks danced before my eyes.

I croaked:

"There's no one here, you know, there's no need for you to go to the trouble…"

"Even so, I'll take a look."

It was no good. The man was one of those who go by the book.

I slipped away down the weed-strewn garden path. When I was clear of the gate I began to run towards my car like a maniac. My heart felt as if it had broken free of its moorings and was jumping about inside my chest like a pea in a whistle.

I didn't have much of a head start over the policeman. Four minutes from now he'd find the two corpses and then all hell would break loose.

I drove back to Paris like the wind. I left the car in a lock-up garage which I rented by the month from a coal merchant and went to ground in my studio.

I had some whisky left in a cupboard. I finished it, straight from the bottle. The alcohol only made me feel even more nauseous. I had to lie down on my divan and close my eyes to calm the dizziness which was making me feeling sick.

I remained for a long time lost in that self-imposed night, grappling with a host of alarming thoughts. Eventually they stopped going round and round in my head and I regained control of myself.

There was no point now in waiting for the birth certificate to arrive or trying to obtain the forged passport. There wasn't a moment to lose. Marianne's description would be circulated. The inspector would provide mine at the same time and that would be the end. Of course, I was in no real danger, but she risked losing everything.

The Spanish authorities would be given her description because unfortunately she'd talked to people about going to

Spain. In Barcelona, a connection would be made between the missing person notification and the statements I'd given… So I needed to get back to her by whatever means it took and find her a hiding place in Spain where she'd be safe… If I didn't, it would be jail for her… or a padded cell.

I almost went straight out and got my car. Then I told myself the registration number would be circulated and be a serious handicap in Spain. Instead I lifted the receiver of my telephone and bought myself a seat on the Barcelona flight. The voice at the other end asked me for my passport number. As I read it out, I felt myself turn pale: I needed a new visa, and that would take time.

I rushed out into the street. I raced off to my bank and withdrew all the money in my account. I had no idea as yet how I'd get it through customs, and was relying on the inspiration of the moment to see me through.

The house in the Rue des Gros-Murs and its ghastly occupants wasn't the issue now. Imminent danger was snapping at my heels. I only had a few hours to play with. Once they were up, it'd be too late. Furnished with my entire savings, I went to the Spanish consulate. It was crowded. I sent my card up to the consul, mentioning that I'd been sent by Jaime Galhardo, leader of the new school of Spanish painting.

He saw me at once, and was very helpful. I told him that I'd just come from Spain, that I'd left my fiancée there and that a telegram had informed me that she'd been taken ill with peritonitis during the night. I needed to get back to her, but I for that needed a new visa and…

Three hours later, I was taking my seat on the plane.

# PART FOUR

# 20

It was a superb night in Barcelona. The lights of the city pitted the ground below us and formed a vast design etched in pin-pricks of fire.

On my left I could see the sea, pale and glinting as far as the eye could see. I felt relief. This was Spain, noble and impassioned, which awaited me and brought me reassurance.

At the airport there were buses for Barcelona. But since Castelldefels lay in the opposite direction and wasn't very far away, I got a private hire car to drive me there. I had all my money intact. To get it through, I'd slipped it inside the pages of a fat magazine which I'd tucked casually under one arm.

The car ferrying me back was an old wreck, a model of a French make of the kind still seen in parts of rural France, with the rear in the form of a flat bed which makes it a delivery van. As we drove I felt the full force of all the pot-holes in the main road. As we approached the Casa Patricio an unbearable feeling of apprehension swelled inside me. I don't mind admitting that I was scared. Scared of seeing her again, knowing who she was or at least who she used to be. I knew that she was a criminal. Or a homicidal maniac, which in one sense was worse.

I thought of the way she looked in my portrait of her. It was strange how my artistic eye unconsciously picked out what had escaped my plain man's eye. I thought back to the day on the beach when she'd torn the wing off the insect... Was it an instinct which lay dormant in her and prompted her to commit such cruel acts?

I'd got that far in my appalling dilemma when my old heap turned off into the bumpy road that led to the beach.

The driver pulled up near the bamboo lean-to. I paid him. I picked up my case and, without bothering to reply to his goodbye, I headed for the Casa.

I saw her, but she didn't see me first. She was sitting at the end of the terrace by a very large fleshy-leafed plant. She was wearing a red skirt which I'd bought for her. She was leaning her chin on her knees and her arms were clasped around her ankles. She was staring out at the leaden sea and not moving. I'd never seen her look more beautiful. The gentle night breeze tugged at her fair hair. Señora Rodriguez sat knitting on the terrace, whiling away the time until the following Saturday which would bring a man to her bed. Not far away from them Tejero was sitting directly on the ground intoning a song of heartbreak and Mister Gin proceeded with his dignified drinker's ritual in the deserted dining hall.

I stepped on a twig and Marianne turned her head and the moon shone directly down on her face. It was as if it were being illuminated by some unearthly light.

"Daniel!"

She staggered with the joy of it. Her teeth chattered as if the full weight of a Siberian winter had just descended on her.

Suddenly, the stench of her house left me. I'd been carrying it around with me like a ghastly putrefying carcass since that morning. Yes, everything was now pure, washed clean, fresh… just like her, the Marianne she once was… An unspoilt girl! Do you understand what I'm saying?

I dropped my case onto the thick, thorny leaves fallen from the succulents… I held her close… I didn't want to think of anything else. I was back with her and she was exactly as she'd been when I'd left, and that was all that mattered.

"Marianne…"

I fed on her lips, her teeth scraped on mine, her breath inflamed my face… The smell of her—her gentle, womanly fragrance—brought to me a redemption I hadn't even dared hope for.

"How did you get back?"

"By plane."

"You couldn't go on living without me, is that it?"

"Yes, Marianne, that's it."

"Oh, my love…"

We didn't have the strength to laugh or cry. Our happiness was so complete that a great golden silence settled on us.

Tejero got up with a grunt. He nodded to me with his dismal look of someone who couldn't have cared less.

With one hand he made the sign that means eating and grafted a silent question mark onto it. I was reminded that I hadn't eaten anything all day and realized I was shaking with hunger.

"Yes, Tejero…"

He produced cold fritters which I found delicious. There was tenderness in Marianne's eyes as she watched me eating.

"Did you get the documents?"

I lied.

"I've set it up… They'll be sent to me."

"When are we going to leave?"

"Soon…"

As I ate, I gazed at her. Was it really possible that this magnificent creature could be a criminal?

Now that my initial burst of happiness had faded, the scent of danger returned.

I couldn't live with her in a state of ecstasy while waiting for the inevitable blow to fall. I knew that if in her former life she'd been driven to murder, no trace of her past actions remained in her. She'd freed herself from them. They'd fallen from her like rotten fruit from the tree. Now new blood flowed through her veins… The problem was that the police wouldn't take her rebirth into account.

Even now they were weaving the giant web with which they'd capture a murderess. The newspapers would be having a field day. She'd be acquitted of killing Bridon, but she wouldn't be forgiven for the death of her child. They'd probably call her the Wicked Mother of Saint-Germain, the Ogress, or something along those lines.

By flying to Spain I had stretched the space separating me from the police. By the time things really started moving on this side of the Pyrenees, I could count on a breathing space of at least forty-eight hours… Every minute counted… I wanted to get out of there at once, but then had second thoughts. I had no means of transport. Besides, I could hardly drag Marianne away in the middle of the night without giving her an explanation.

I summoned Tejero with a wave of my hand… He came, shuffling in his fraying rope sandals.

"*Mañana Montserrat…*"

It was the standard excursion, the one all the tourists staying in and around Barcelona went on.

"*Si…*"

I told him that my car had broken down and that the *patron* would be taking us to the station very early.

"*Si…*"

Once that was settled I stood up, and Marianne followed me into my room.

She sat down on my bed. There wasn't much space in that cell, which made this necessary. She was expecting me to go to her, but I didn't want her. I loved her with a love that was more spiritual than before, a love more chaste than at the start of our life together.

"Are you worried about something, Daniel?"

She was looking at me with a surprised, forlorn expression on her face.

"I'm tired, darling." I said. "Please try to understand…"

"Yes, of course… Well, in that case, we shouldn't go on any excursions tomorrow…"

"But we should…"

"Wouldn't we be better staying here, on the beach, the two of us?"

The mere thought of it made me feel nothing but misery. I was utterly wretched at the prospect of having to leave the Casa Patricio.

"Listen, Marianne, I want us to get away from here… Don't ask me why, I'll explain later…"

She'd have liked to press the point but then, seeing my poor careworn face, she desisted.

The violin was out of its case. She followed the direction of my gaze…

"When you were away, I used to come in here and play. It was a wonderful way of being near you."

She picked up the instrument. I pictured the shabby drawing room in the Rue des Gros-Murs, the jaws of the lion on the hasp, the net curtains…

"Not now, Marianne!"

She put the violin back. When she turned and faced me, tears were glistening in her eyes.

"Daniel," she stammered, "don't you… don't you love me any more?"

It was inevitable that she'd say that. But my God, yes, I loved her! I loved her more than my sanity, loved her so much I could have died for love of her… Yes! Died of love. It wasn't until that moment that I truly understood the meaning of the expression.

I threw myself on her like a wild thing. I tore off her skirt, her blouse… and crucified her there, on that bed.

# 21

Recovering from the intensity of our passionate embrace, we lay like two effigies on a tomb. The Casa had fallen silent and the pulsating sea had resumed its dominion over the universe... From time to time Tricornio, the yellow dog, bayed at the moon. Through the window I had an inverted view of a blue sky which didn't look at all like the heavens at night. I experienced a sense of security, for I was lulled by the sound of the Mediterranean. It gave me a comforting feeling, as if I were a living being lost in the ends of the earth, in a land beyond the reach of danger.

Marianne began to speak.

"Don't you know, Daniel?"

Her voice had come from very far away. It seemed as if I were hearing it through glass.

"Know what?"

"That when I play the violin my memory comes back."

"What did you say?"

I leant over her. My teeth were clenched so hard that my jaws started hurting like blazes.

"What's wrong?" she stammered... "Daniel! You're scaring me... Your eyes, they frighten me!... They're bloodshot!..."

Blood! The poor girl's hands were steeped in it. And she didn't know.

"I'm sorry, Marianne, but I love you so much you could say I'm jealous of your past life."

"Jealous?"

"Yes, isn't that idiotic?"

"No, I understand..."

She put her arms around my neck.

"You know, it's not important, because I haven't remembered much."

"What do you remember?"

She closed her eyes so that she could concentrate.

"Well now... You know about the window with the lion's jaws?"

"Yes, Marianne, I know."

"And outside there's the branch..."

"Yes..."

"Well, if I go closer, I can see a swing hanging from a tree... Isn't that strange?"

"It's because there was a swing there, Marianne... And next, what do you see next?"

"I see a woman with a red face walking past and she looks up and smiles at me..."

Immediately I thought: "her mother".

"And is that all?"

"No... I can hear something too."

"What exactly do you hear?"

"As I play, there's a child crying somewhere above my head."

I closed my eyes. A sick feeling was rising in my gorge.

"And it interferes with my playing..."

"Really?"

"Yes... and each time I hear it I stumble over the score... I can't make it out... The hand holding the bow shakes."

I noticed the perspiration standing on her forehead. She was reliving these snatches of her past so powerfully that they left her literally drained.

"Can you see anything else?"

"No..."

114

"Well, just try and forget it… Don't force it…"

"Yes, Daniel…"

"Don't think of anything except us, all right?"

"There's nothing I want more…"

I kissed her and eventually we both slept. Just before being swallowed up in those healing depths, she reached for my hand.

I shivered, because her hand was as cold as death.

# 22

When I woke, my watch said seven o'clock... It was time to leave. I had a large beach bag into which I'd put my alpaca suit. After I'd shaved I put on a pair of cotton slacks and a blue sweater. Then I stuffed my money into my travel case and the case into the bag. Next, I shook Marianne.

"On your feet, lazybones..."

When she slept she looked even more angelic than when her big blue eyes were on me. It seemed such a shame to wake her.

She gave a sigh, and a little smile spread over her face.

"You're here, Daniel?"

"Yes, my darling..."

"Cross your heart?"

"Look!"

She opened her eyes.

"Thank you."

We'd started the day exactly as if we were really going on an outing, whereas in fact we were running away.

I'd been right not to use my own car, but not having a vehicle was inconvenient. I'd got into the habit of using my car the way I used my legs, and I felt handicapped without it.

Old man Patricio drove us to the station in his little three-wheeled delivery van.

As he was about to set off back, he asked:

"This evening?"

"No. *Mañana!*"

I pointed to my easel, which I was taking with me...

"Painting… Montserrat!"

"*Si*…"

Then came the usual daily handshake, and the thread was broken. Marianne and I were two fugitives, only she didn't know it.

Instead of getting the train for Barcelona, as we should have done if we were really going to Montserrat, we came back out of the station and got onto the bus for Sitges.

"Aren't we taking the train?" Marianne said in surprise.

"No, I was just thinking that it's all twists and zigzags by train, it stops every time it comes to a bend in the track… It'll be better if we take a bus…"

When we reached Sitges, I managed to find another bus for Vendrell. From there we got on a third bus, to Tarragona. Marianne's surprise got bigger and bigger.

At one point, when we were inside a coach station, she stopped in front of a map of Spain fixed to a wall.

She turned to me. Her face was pale.

"Look, Daniel, we're going the wrong way for Montserrat…"

"Who cares!… We'll go there some other time… I think it's nicer along the coast, don't you?"

"Yes… but do we have to keep getting on all these buses? It'll mean a great trek getting back to Casa Patricio."

The time had come to bring things into the open.

"Listen, Marianne, I have a confession to make…"

It threw her completely. I saw real panic in her eyes.

"I…"

"Tell me straight, it's about me, isn't it?"

I shook my head.

"No, Marianne. It's about me… A few years ago I was involved in politics in France… extremist politics… As you

117

know, this country is a dictatorship. I've heard that the authorities here have got their eye on me. I could be deported. I don't want that to happen before I receive the documents which will allow me to take you with me. Have you got that?"

"Of course! So?"

"So in the meantime we're going to find ourselves a quiet corner somewhere and hide out."

She seemed to fall for my story. I was quite pleased with my little scheme.

We'd already taken our seats in the third bus when suddenly Marianne gave a start.

"But... Daniel!"

"What?"

"How are we going to get the documents if we leave the Casa Patricio without notifying anybody?"

I was caught on the hop.

She looked alarmed and I had to come up with something plausible fast to set her mind at rest.

"Don't worry. I told them to hold the documents in France until I forward the address of a place to send them."

"Oh, I see..."

And then we started to talk about something else.

# 23

It was midday when we got to Tarragona. I was beginning to feel the effects of my exertions of the previous day. I told myself there was no point in running all the way to the other end of Spain. What I had to do was find a hiding place which was safe, and that could be anywhere. When we were holed up, I'd wait until things calmed down and then find a way of returning to France. I hadn't yet reached the stage of thinking that my involvement could compromise my career or even land me in jail, because I was willingly aiding and abetting a murderess. If only that stupid oaf of a policeman hadn't had the unhelpful idea of turning up in the Rue des Gros-Murs at the very moment when I was there, I would have stayed out of the case altogether and that would have avoided a great many complications. Still, there was no point crying over spilt milk. I had better things to do.

We sat down at a table on the terrace of a café and, as I sipped my sherry, I allowed myself a moment to take stock of the situation.

If we found a room in a hotel or even a simple village inn, we'd be taking a big risk because given the number of *carabineros* who'd be combing the whole of Spain, we wouldn't remain at large for three days once they had our descriptions.

I had an idea: we could rent a small house where we could hide without attracting attention. I told Marianne to wait for me, and got up and started walking through the town. I began by converting some of my money at a bureau de change, then I went looking for a rentals agency. I found one in the town centre. In the window were numerous photographs which had faded in the sun. They all showed buildings for sale or for rent in the area. I went in.

A tall young woman who was running to fat spoke to me in French. This disconcerted me.

"How did you know I was French?"

"I used to live in Paris."

And she smiled at me.

"I'd like to rent a small house, not too expensive, for a month."

"I have just the thing for you!"

She opened a filing cabinet and took out a pink index card to which a photograph was attached with a paperclip.

"Would this suit you?"

It was a detached house, all white, surrounded by palm trees.

"Hardly. Wouldn't this be more suitable for a Hollywood star?"

"It's suitable for anyone with ten thousand pesetas to spend!"

I did the sum in my head. It was the equivalent of about 700 French francs. It was nothing! So, for a very small outlay, you could give the impression that you were a big shot.

I produced the ten thousand pesetas.

"Since today is the twenty-fourth," the blowzy girl said, "you're entitled to a bonus of six extra days. I'll give you a post-dated receipt in order to start the rental period from the first day of next month."

"Thanks."

"Here are the keys. The house is thirteen kilometres from here, not far from the sea. Obviously, if the house was next to the beach, the price would be higher."

I wasn't too bothered about the beach. There are too many people on beaches.

She wrote the address on the back of the receipt.

"You can get a taxi to take you there…"

Which is exactly what we did. You have to admit, you don't usually get to rent a house as quickly as that and then make a beeline for it with the keys in your pocket.

We were both in seventh heaven. We rediscovered childish enthusiasms and the sense of wonder which slumbers permanently in the human heart.

She asked questions about the photo I'd been shown.

"And you said it's really beautiful?"

"A place fit for millionaires!"

When we got there we were brought down to earth with a bump. The house stood a little too near an ugly road in a featureless landscape. Moreover, the photo I'd seen must have been taken the day they'd finished building the house.

It had aged considerably since then. Wide cracks zigzagged across the grey façade, and the garden plants had spread everywhere. The palm trees were lanky and yellow… The whole place reeked of sun-scorched, quiet desperation.

We looked at each other.

"Not exactly a palace of delights, is it?"

She shrugged her shoulders.

"What does it matter, now that we're together?"

"You're right."

We watched the taxi disappear in a monstrous cloud of white dust. I pushed the ramshackle gate through which we reached the path leading to the front door.

And so we moved into our new house with possessions consisting of just an easel, a paint box and a beach bag. Our adventure wasn't entirely without its funny side.

As I got to the door of the villa I stopped, struck by the resemblance it bore to that other house, the one in the Rue des

Gros-Murs. There was virtually no difference between them, even down to the overgrown vegetation around it.

"What's the matter?" asked Marianne.

"Does this house remind you of anything?"

She stared at it.

"No, why?"

"Oh, nothing… I… I always have a feeling that any new sight might reawaken something in you…"

"Well, you're wrong…"

I opened the front door. Here, unlike in the other place, there was no smell of damp. The walls gave out a pleasant odour of hot stone.

"Shall we move in?"

"Sure!"

Basically, the fact that the house was isolated was a bonus for us. The nearest village was two kilometres away. I now knew why the rent was so low.

The way the rooms were laid out also recalled the internal arrangement of the other house. On the right, a drawing room furnished in the modern Spanish style—that is, with atrocious taste. On the left, a kitchen. A staircase at the far end, painted white, and on the first floor two bedrooms.

"Come on, let's take a look at our bed!"

She snuggled up close to me.

"I really have the feeling that we're already at home, Daniel!"

"But we are at home!"

With our arms around each other, we climbed the stairs. She reached out one hand for the handle of the door on the right. Suddenly as she was about to turn it, she gave a terrible scream, a scream which rang through the empty house. She trembled like a leaf in the wind. I supported her… As she seemed to be passing out, I kicked the door open so that I could lay her down somewhere. But she sobbed:

"No! No!"

She dug in her heels to stop me making her go into the room. I had to grab her around the waist. We went through the door. The room was all white and full of sunshine, with a low bed and furniture rather less kitsch than on the ground floor. Marianne calmed down instantly. She passed one hand over her perspiring forehead.

"What was the matter, darling?"

She shook her head.

"It was terrifying."

I was bathed in sweat and my need to yell and scream was as great as hers. I asked questions for form's sake, but I knew what this was all about: the door at the top of the stairs had suddenly reminded her of that other bedroom...

"As I opened the door, it seemed to me that I'd find dead people inside..."

"What an idea!"

"Yes... it came to me in a flash. I saw blood... bodies laid out..."

"And did it remind you of anything?"

"No, it was just an image... You know, a nightmare!"

I told myself that nightmares belonged to the world of sleep. Not once since I'd discovered the ghastly truth had I envisaged the possibility that Marianne might recover her memory. The thought of it seemed so monstrous.

What would I do if she suddenly called out: "I remember everything!"?

I rushed down the stairs to fetch her some water from the kitchen, but the pump at the sink hadn't been primed. I was beginning to feel rather less proud of "my" house.

A few hundred metres before reaching the house, I'd noticed a drinking fountain by the side of the road. I grabbed the handle of a bucket and went off in pursuit of water. As I walked, very dark thoughts rolled round inside my head. The isolation of the place made it somehow depressing. It didn't really look like Spain at all, but resembled rather an Australian desert, being flat, seemingly endless and stippled with dry, black, stunted trees. What had the man who'd built this poky little house in this out-of-the-way spot been thinking of?

The sun was beating down. I was returning with my bucket full of water when two *carabineros* on bicycles overtook me. They gave me rather surprised looks but didn't stop.

At that moment I couldn't prevent myself from thinking that if there is a hell it must be like my life at that moment. A sinister, scorching location… A gloomy house… And a woman who was beautiful and pure but also a criminal… That was the fact of it.

I put the bucket down for a moment, scooped up water in both cupped hands and splashed it on my face.

When I got back I shouted "hello!" but no one answered. Seized by sudden panic I took the stairs at a run. Marianne was sleeping crosswise on the bed. On her unconscious face two tears still glistened in the sun.

## 24

When it was evening we went out to buy provisions in the village. It was a typical Mediterranean village with bleached roofs and shops with quaint displays of goods. They didn't have front windows, just an opening in a wall, and everywhere a jumble of hams, brooms, baskets of fruit and wine in goatskin bottles.

Marianne had completely got over that morning's episode. I avoided the subject so as not to upset her, but it had undermined the strange happiness I'd been feeling. She'd been the young murderess who was being sought by the French police. To me, she was a different person altogether who had no connection with the other one from Saint-Germain. But now the shock had in some way reunited those two distinct women. For just a brief moment, it is true, but a repetition of the same phenomenon was now a real threat to us, since it had already happened once.

We'd bought a stack of shopping and we were loaded like donkeys as we walked back to the villa. The evening shadows were deepening, for we hadn't set out until it was late in the afternoon. The dry landscape was turning yellow with a greenish edge to it. It was an interesting colour, but I had no "feel" for it. I found it slightly oppressive.

As we went on our way I saw in the distance the same two *carabineros* who were coming back from their patrol.

"This way!" I said to Marianne.

Nearby was a stand of thorny cactus. We crouched down behind it.

Not moving a muscle, not speaking and avoiding each other's eye, we waited for the two men to pass.

"Right, let's go!"

She got to her feet and picked up the net bag full of fruit which she'd been carrying. She looked thoughtful.

"Daniel," she said, coming to a sudden stop in the middle of the road, "I have this feeling that you're hiding something from me."

"You're joking!"

"Unfortunately I'm not… You're not going to make me believe you've got to avoid the first policeman that comes along because you used to be involved in politics in France!"

"But I assure you—"

"I'm sorry, I don't believe you. If you really were an undesirable, they wouldn't have given you a visa!"

Feminine logic was gaining the upper hand. I felt on the defensive.

"Anyway," she went on, "you weren't scared of policemen before you went on your short trip to France. You even used to have a drink with the ones who came to the Casa Patricio!"

This argument overcame any inclination I had to lie. She let the grapes and peaches drop onto the dusty earth and grabbed me by my sweater with both hands.

"It's all on my account, I can feel it!"

"You're crazy!"

It's a very common expression. She lowered her eyes.

"Maybe I am."

"Oh come on, Marianne, I wasn't serious!"

"No. I've been thinking a lot about my condition. If I can lose my memory after being involved in a very minor car accident, I couldn't have had a very solid brain to start with, wouldn't you say?"

"That's got nothing to do with it... It's a kind of... of inexplicable phenomenon..."

"Perhaps, but you still haven't answered my question. It's on my account that you've gone into hiding, isn't it?"

I felt so much at a loss that I was on the point of telling her everything, of throwing the truth in her face like a bucket of dirty water. But I got a grip on myself. No, I couldn't do that to her. Whatever the cost, I had to go on lying.

"I'm going to tell you the truth."

"Go ahead, tell it!"

"As I was coming back, I killed somebody with my car, somewhere near Gerona. An old man who was crossing the road. I said to myself that I'd be arrested and..."

She shook her head. I couldn't believe I'd got into a fix like this. I kept spouting lies to spare her the truth and here she was, a murderess, who was questioning me calmly, coolly, with all the tenacity of an experienced policeman.

"They don't arrest people for being in a car accident. Or at least, not for long. You're lying!"

Her cheeks were red and her eyes were fixed and staring. Her hands were still clutching my sweater and I could feel her nails digging into my flesh."

"I want the truth, Daniel. And if you love me, you'll tell me! Out with it, you found out something about me!"

"What could I possibly discover about you that would make me need to hide you?"

This thought stopped her in her tracks. She lowered her hands and let them hang at the sides of skirt.

"That's true... Unless... Tell me, Daniel, I was married, wasn't I? And my husband is looking for me, is that it?"

"No..."

"Did I do something bad... before?"

I couldn't take any more. No questioning of a suspect was ever tougher than this.

"Of course not! Anyway, how would I know?"

"I thought... It was that flashback I had this morning... The blood... You don't think I could have really seen it and..."

"Stop torturing yourself, that way you really will go crazy, my lovely. But since you really want the truth, here it is: I'm wanted by the French police."

"What did you do?"

"Fraud..."

"You're lying, you're much too honest for that. You'd be incapable of harming anybody."

"I'd made a copy of a Matisse, for my own amusement... An art collector came to my studio, noticed it and just as a boast I told him it was an original. He wanted to buy it from me... I'd had enough of going hungry. So I seized the opportunity. He paid me a lot of money for it and that's how I managed to get to Spain. The other day, when I was in France, I read in a newspaper that I was wanted on a charge of forgery and embezzlement... I came back straight away... Oh, not to escape justice, but so that I wouldn't lose you!"

I looked at her. I didn't know if she was going to believe me this time, but I had given it my best shot: my voice was so convincing that I was moved myself. My fake confession gave me a guilt complex. She believed the whole story. Her face was strained, disapproving.

"Did you really do that?"

"Yes, but..."

"You, a painter, you abused your talent to extract money?"

"Listen, Marianne!"

"Thief!"

If I'd been struck by lightning, I wouldn't have been more stunned. She stood there, heaping abuse on me, spitting her contempt in my face.

"Marianne!"

"Liar!"

"But..."

"You've just told me three lies, one after the other. I never thought you were like that!... Oh my God!"

She flung herself face down on the scrubby roadside bank and hiccupped several times. I didn't have the strength to try and help. Only the full truth, which is to say her truth, would have absolved me in her eyes. And I didn't have the right to speak it to her.

So I waited until she calmed down. And calm down she did, little by little.

In a curt voice I asked:

"Are you all right now?"

She nodded a "yes".

"Let's go back, then."

I was really furious with her and with myself. I picked up her net of fruit and set off towards the house. She walked by my side, swinging her arms. The slap of her Grecian sandals on the dusty road filled my head like a hammer's pounding.

# 25

We'd eaten very little and exchanged only a few words. We had nothing to say to each other. By lying, I'd created a truth which she found intolerable. I'd have to wait. Inwardly, I cursed myself for a fool. I should have come up with some other explanation. I had tried, it's true, but I had failed.

It goes without saying that the electricity wasn't working in the villa. Lightning had struck the connecting cable that ran across the property and no one had bothered to come out to fix it. All things considered, the house was worth nothing, and the figure of 10,000 pesetas for renting it now looked prohibitively steep.

We lighted our way up to bed with matches. We fumbled to undress in the dark. She curled up in a ball on her side of the bed and deliberately turned her back on me.

I wanted her very badly, but I held back. I knew she'd have pushed me away and I couldn't have borne being rebuffed by Marianne. I lay for a long time in the dark, bitterly mulling over my grievances. It was obvious to me that fate was conspiring against me. I'd been caught up in a macabre vortex. With every step I took I became more entangled in invisible threads.

In the end I slipped into a clammy sleep. I was hot, I was uncomfortable... I saw Bridon's decomposing corpse swirling round and round me, as if trapped in the eddies of a whirlpool.

I kept thinking that perhaps she'd kill me as I slept. She could at any time succumb to a fit of madness. I wasn't afraid of dying. I accepted it. Coming from her hands, death would be a gift of great price.

I was woken by a sensation of extreme heat and became aware that I was lying in a pool of the sunshine which was flooding through the window.

I rolled over into the middle of the bed. I was expecting to feel Marianne's body against my bare skin, but all I found were the two sheets one on top of the other. They were now together and my knee reached out in vain, sliding between them but encountering nothing.

I opened my eyes. She wasn't there. I leapt out of bed. The chair on which she'd thrown her things was empty. I hopped about on the wooden floor without managing to get into my clothes. I kept muttering disconnected words in a whining voice. They still echo in my memory.

Eventually I was dressed. I was about to leave the room when I saw something odd on the table. She'd emptied a matchbox and used its contents to form the word "ADIEU".

All my fears were confirmed. The silly little fool had gone… She'd run away from me because she believed I was a crook!

I wondered if she'd been gone long. My watch said eight o'clock. I'd heard nothing, felt nothing.

I ran outside. A kind of translucent haze hovered at ground level. As far as my eyes could see, all I could make out was dreary, empty countryside with its skeletal vegetation.

I had no idea in which direction I should go… I didn't have a car… My God, it was scary as hell!

I checked to see if she'd taken any money from our stash, but she hadn't. All my pesetas were still there in my travel case.

Marianne had gone without any money, without a plan… She'd just run away from me.

Instead of making for the village nearby, I set off at a run towards the town, through a landscape of gravel and sand. I walked quickly, shoulders hunched, looking desperately for Marianne's tracks on the stony ground.

There was nothing… So then I began to run straight ahead like a lost soul calling her name. I refused to accept the obvious. She couldn't have gone!… She couldn't have left me!… Any moment now one of those swine in the three-cornered hats would arrest her… No, I had to find her, whatever the cost. And quickly! It was a hunt with no quarter given… The Spanish police were innumerable and everywhere… And there was me, who was doubtless also being hunted, I, who didn't speak a word of Spanish and had only my two feeble legs.

"Marianne! Mariaaaanne!"

The ceaseless buzzing of insects was all the answer I got.

# PART FIVE

## 26

I ran for hours. I'd stop when I met someone to ask if he or she had seen Marianne. I spoke in a kind of pigeon Spanish, but such was my determination to find her that I managed to make myself understood almost as well as if I'd had a perfect command of the language of Cervantes.

The replies were always the same:

"No…"

No sign of Marianne… I'd been going in the wrong direction… So I turned and went back, taking short cuts to go faster… I came within sight of sweltering hamlets… I grabbed peasants by the lapels of their jackets:

*"Una señorita con cabellos dorados!"*

None of them had ever seen a girl with golden hair… There were very few of them in those parts.

They gave me suspicious looks, obviously thinking that I was mad.

I have no idea how long my fruitless pursuit through that depressing landscape lasted. My rope sandals began to unravel. As I walked now, I dragged my feet.

"It's over," I told myself… "completely over… I'll never find her."

I made my way slowly back to the villa to collect my documents, my money and my paints and easel. It took me several hours to find the place because of the many switches in direction I'd made.

When I finally saw it on the horizon, looking grey and depressing crouching among those yellowed palm trees, I was staggering with exhaustion.

The last few metres were the most painful. My leaden legs refused to work. I stumbled against the broken-down gate in the fence and had to lean on a stunted bush to gather together the last of my strength. In the end, I just about made the short distance to the house.

From the doorway, I saw her. She was in the living room, sitting at the table, with both hands clasped in front of her. She watched me come in without moving.

I was at the end of my tether.

"You little bitch!"

I pulled up the chair facing her and sank onto it with paralytic slowness. We glared at each other and slowly I felt my resentment fade. I was happy to see her again. My chest and throat were racked by a series of dry sobs.

"You're trembling!" she said softly.

"I've run miles and called your name over and over... Why did you come back?"

"Because I love you too much, Daniel... Nothing can ever separate me from you."

"So why did you go?"

"I woke up, very early, and I watched you sleeping... And I really believed you were a thief. I felt ashamed... I didn't think I could stay by your side any more!"

"You silly girl!"

"Yes, I know... That's what I kept telling myself as I walked. My love should be above all that..."

She stood up, walked round the table and knelt at my feet. She took my hands in hers. I felt her lovely soft face against my fingers.

"I shan't ever be angry with you again, Daniel. I forgive you."

I closed my eyes and somewhere in deep within me a secret voice murmured:

"And I forgive you!"

That evening we spent in the villa at the world's end was the most extraordinary of my entire life. Are there words capable of expressing the fierceness of our embraces, our animal cries, our tears and above all our unbridled determination to belong to each other body and soul, come hell or high water!

There were brief interludes of fevered sleep and then we'd fling ourselves at each other again and again, as if by bonding so completely we were attempting to forge a new entity that was stronger than existence itself… As if our union freed us from life, from its shackles and its dangers.

In the end, a little before the first light of dawn, we plunged into the pit of nothingness.

I hadn't wound my watch for some time, and when I woke it had stopped. But judging by the strength of the heat and the position of the sun I thought it must be getting on for noon. I could have eaten a horse. I went down to the kitchen to make *café au lait* and carried two breakfast bowls plus toast to our room.

Marianne had just opened her eyes. She seemed rather disorientated, which made me feel slightly anxious.

"Something wrong, darling?"

"Not really, it's just that I had bad dreams last night. I think it was all the commotion yesterday that caused them."

I set the steaming bowls of coffee down on the table where the word "ADIEU" was still picked out in matchsticks.

"What sort of dreams were they, Marianne?"

She lowered her eyes. Her long blonde hair cascaded in a golden rain over her shoulders, leaving her tanned breasts, so admirably proportioned and firm, fully exposed…

In a voice crackling with anxiety, I repeated:

"What sort of bad dreams?"

Would what she was about to say frighten me out of my wits?

"I saw a white cradle, drifting down a river. In it was a dead child… It floated on until it was sucked down by a whirlpool!"

The moronic snicker I managed to produce was the most pitiful response anyone ever heard.

"Well, as nightmares go…"

I held out her *café au lait* to her. She stirred it mechanically.

"Daniel…"

"Yes?"

"You don't think that… that I had a child, *before*?"

"What a strange idea!"

I had a feeling that her memory would come back gradually… There was something slowly working away in her, and when it had restored a sufficient number of images to her troubled brain she'd remember everything. And her new life would run seamlessly into the old.

The prospect of that happening frightened me much more then the police.

"All the same," she sighed, "dreaming about such strange things isn't exactly normal."

"Strangeness is the stuff of dreams, Marianne…"

Bringing her to this isolated villa had been a mistake. The moment I walked in I'd sensed instantly that I was surrounded by an atmosphere similar to that of the house at Saint-Germain. In this life, atmosphere is everything. The extraordinary aura of this house had stirred her sleeping memory.

I had to do something, find a way of slowing this reversion to the past.

I'd have to put all my intelligence, all my love, all my determination to work.

"Listen, Marianne, this is ridiculous. Do you intend to identify with every silly dream you have? Let's say that one night you dream about a bearded lady. Are you going to conclude that in your previous life you were in a freak show at the fair?"

That barely raised a smile... She didn't move, she didn't eat.

"Daniel, if I did have a child, I wouldn't have forgotten, would I?"

"Hardly!"

"Surely I'd feel it in my bones?"

"But of course, obviously..."

It was only now that she felt the maternal instinct. She'd allowed her small son to die but now she knew the true value of a child.

"Daniel..."

"Marianne?..."

"I'd like us to have a child. Would you like that too?"

At this point I had the feeling that I was opening that door on the first floor of the house in the Rue des Gros-Murs.

Again I had the reek of the charnel house in my nose, I could sense the presence of the two dead bodies. The corpse of the old man, mutilated, sliced open, oozing blood... And the child's body covered with putrefying matter.

For the first time, she filled me with horror. Not for what she'd done, but because of the ties which bound her to those two deaths. I was thinking of that naked old man who'd lain on top of her... I was thinking of that small filthy, festering child which had been born of their ignoble union. The thought of it made my flesh creep. I felt I'd reached the very bottom of the sink of human depravity.

We finished our breakfast. It was a sad time, because we had nothing to say.

Marianne put her bowl down.

"What shall we do today?"

The question took me by surprise. In this place, there was nothing to do... It was just desert, no sea or lake, no sports to play, no interesting walks... All we could do was wander along white dusty paths, tripping over rocks and watching out for the milky-white leaves covered with treacherous spines of the exotic plant life.

"We'll do some painting..."

"We?"

"Yes... I want to paint your portrait again..."

"Why?"

"Because you're a subject that inspires me, that's why."

I was determined to paint her picture again, in the light of what I now knew. The first time I had unwittingly stressed what wasn't right about her... Her homicidal madness gleamed in her eye, and I couldn't recall having consciously tried to convey it... I didn't remember the exact shade of light blue for it that I'd applied to the canvas. Now I was going to have to paint her pure, blameless essence while all the time knowing that she'd committed criminal acts and that she carried the germ of it within her.

"All right... Since you feel inspired..."

It was the ideal solution since it allowed us to kill time without our being aware of it.

I painted for a good part of the day, but I wasn't happy with my work because that cruel look in her eye kept reappearing, although I did my best to forget it. I couldn't see it when I looked at Marianne, but it was there on the canvas: ineradicable, persistent, invasive, blotting out all the other expressions of her face.

When we stopped for a break Marianne came to take a look at the canvas.

"Why have you made me look so cross?"

I didn't answer.

I tried to retouch some of what I'd sketched out. I lost the likeness… The portrait became an anonymous picture… I was forced to accept the obvious: I was painting Marianne, which meant that I was painting a murderess, and there was nothing I could do about it…

Utterly dismayed by the sorcery of my art, I abandoned the picture. We'd run out of bread. I suggested to Marianne that we could go to the bakery but she said no, because she was feeling tired. So I set out alone to walk to the small village. I was glad to get away for a while from that bewitched house and even more so from the enchantments of Marianne. My love was such a strange thing. First and foremost it was physical attraction and the "graphic" attraction, if I can express it so. I loved her body, her symmetry, the smell of her, the way she looked at me… I loved her mystery.

I wanted to save her. It wasn't her fault if she'd been dumped on a dung heap with a violin for a soul.

I had several drinks in the bar in the village. Then I bought bread and some fruit along with a slice of wild boar pâté.

I was about to make my way back when I wondered if anyone sold French newspapers in the locality. I was told I'd have to go to Tarragona to find any. As it happened, the *patron* of the bar was about to go there on an aged motorbike which belched black smoke and made a noise like an air show. He said he'd bring some back for me.

I gave him a hundred-peseta note and asked if he'd deliver them to the villa when he got back.

He arrived just as it was getting dark. Marianne was making a fruit salad over which she poured rum. I had paint all over my hands. I called to the man to put the papers on the table and then showed him to the door.

When I got back to the kitchen Marianne was picking up one of the papers. It was *Le Figaro*. I grabbed the other, *France-Soir*. Marianne's picture was plastered over two columns on the front page. It was a fuzzy passport photo which the police must have come across in a drawer of the old house. What struck me forcefully was that it really made her look like a criminal. Her eyes seemed shifty and a pouting lower lip gave her mouth an unpleasant twist. Her blonde hair, neatly combed and pulled back, emphasized her hard, sly side. It really wasn't her at all. Seeing her in that wretched snapshot, I felt not so much revulsion at what she'd been *before* as admiration for what she'd become *since*. A radical transformation had come about in every aspect of her person. The dominant features of her face had altered.

I looked up and saw that she was holding a newspaper. A newspaper that was about to reveal with brutal directness what I was making so many great sacrifices to hide from her.

I wasted no time.

"Give me that, Marianne!"

I snatched the paper out of her hands. I feverishly scanned the front page: nothing there... Nor on the inside pages either... Then it struck me that I should look at the date on it and saw that the *Figaro* was two days older than the *France-Soir*. I handed it back to her, but she didn't take it.

"Why did you do that, Daniel?"

"So sorry!"

"Anyone would think you were afraid I might read something particular in the paper."

"Do you think that?"

"Yes!"

"It's not that, Marianne, but you're still at the stage of recollecting shadows from the past, and I get nervous and act before I think…"

Tentatively, I added:

"Know what I mean?"

"Yes, I know… But, Daniel, you must realize that my memory will come back."

"What do you mean?"

"I can feel it… I get these clicks in my head. All the time I keep stopping because I see hazy things, it's like looking into a room through misted-up windows."

"And have you seen any new things since this morning?"

"Yes, while you were painting my portrait."

"What did you see?"

She paused to think.

"A house… A hallway… I know that our house was like this one… With a hallway and an upstairs."

"Are you sure?"

"Almost."

"And does this house here help you to remember?"

"Yes…"

"In that case, we must get away!"

"No, Daniel, it's too late now. You see, I want to rid myself of the torment of it. It would be better if I could remember… It wouldn't change the way I feel about you in any way. Whatever people I remember, I'll stay with you! As I told you at Castelldefels: I never loved anyone except you! The closer I get to the truth, the more utterly convinced of that I become!"

I kissed her. Her lips weren't as cool as usual. She had a slight temperature. Yes, there was definitely something going on inside her.

"Just now, Marianne, you said: I know that our house was like this one…"

"So?"

"You said *our*: so you must be aware that you didn't live there by yourself?"

She dug one hand into her hair, dragging her fingers through the honey-coloured thatch which soaked up all the light in the room.

"But it seems to me that I lived there almost alone… Someone had just died… I couldn't get used to it…"

For a moment she listened to some secret murmur coming from deep inside her.

"But no… There was someone…"

She automatically looked upwards—her instinct had conjured up the gesture.

"Someone… upstairs… Someone who wouldn't let me play my violin…"

"You're just imagining it!"

"No!… Wait!"

I was now horribly afraid.

"Stop, Marianne. Stop this now! Put it out of your mind! Do you hear me? I can't stand it! Stop!"

She sat down at the table and resumed chopping up fruit into small pieces into the chipped salad bowl.

I picked up my *France-Soir* and walked to the bottom of the garden to read it.

There at least she was unlikely to burst in on me unexpectedly. I could read in peace... to find out more.

## 27

The paper wasn't kind to her. But it didn't tell me anything I didn't know already. The policeman had found the bodies and there had been a terrific hullabaloo in Saint-Germain. The piece summarized Marianne's life, stressing her depraved past. She was the typical little provincial girl on the make who set out to feather her nest by fluttering her eyelashes at her mother's lover after her death. She'd borne him a child which she'd neglected, preferring to spend her time, so said the journalist, "scraping away at her violin". She had allowed the child to starve to death, and when her elderly lover found out she'd done away with him. This was the police version of events.

No money was found in Bridon's wallet, proof positive that Marianne Renard had robbed her victim before running away. Her description had been widely circulated and it was expected that the "monster" would soon be arrested. The article concluded with the hypothesis that Marianne had a lover and had run away with him. This lover—me—allegedly returned to the house probably to recover some valuable item, and maybe it was he who'd stolen Bridon's money from his wallet. The police were following his trail and hoped that they'd get to Marianne through him.

I tore the paper into very small pieces which I buried at the foot of a palm tree… Then I went back in to join "the monster".

I'd never seen her look more beautiful and more tragic. No one would feel any pity for her: no one! She was a woman beyond the pale. And yet I understood the fuller picture. I could easily imagine a young girl with romantic ideas brought up in that old house by a neurotic mother who was visited by her boorish lover in her home, in front of the girl. She'd used her music to escape reality. All her poetry, all her sentimental fancies had been focused on her bow… Thanks to that bow, the hideous, savage life she led lost its harshness. On the tragic death of her mother, the old man had switched his attentions to her, and she'd submitted because for this fragile soul he represented the demands made by life. He was the unavoidable, the inevitable price she had to pay each and every day… She'd given birth to her baby, I assume, with more surprise and terror than joy… But it hadn't triggered any maternal feeling in her. Gradually, she had—I'm about to use a word that is unthinkable but might well correctly sum up the situation—*forgotten* all about her son. He'd become a vague presence, a nuisance which disturbed the release she found in her violin…

"Why so down in the mouth, Daniel?"

I was going to have to put a brave face on things.

"You keep saying that! I've got things on my mind, that's all…"

"What things?"

"Things I've done!"

"Honest?"

"Honest!"

"Could you go to jail?"

"Definitely!"

She shook her head.

"I don't want them to put you in jail, Daniel. What would I do without you? Tell me! I couldn't go on living."

"No one's going to send me to prison!"

"You really believe that?"

"I promise you…"

"It would be so awful for me… You do see that?"

"Don't let's keep talking about it, Marianne… Anticipating the worst is always more painful than facing it. Right, why not serve up what there is to eat? What's on the menu?"

"Omelette!"

"With eggs in?"

She smiled.

"Yes. Do you like omelettes?"

"I'm crazy about them!"

The omelette smelt good. I watched Marianne busying herself. As a cook, she was about as bungling as the average artist. Domesticity didn't come naturally to her.

When the omelette was ready it looked like anything except an omelette. It was slightly burnt on one side and not browned at all on the other.

Marianne set out two plates. The landlord had left a few chipped items of kitchen ware, just enough to justify calling the villa "furnished".

She brought the frying pan and served me a huge portion of omelette.

"Taste and see how good it is."

I tasted it. She'd forgotten the salt.

"That's really great," I lied. "With just a little pinch of salt it would be perfect."

She put a more modest helping on the other plate. There was still a large amount of omelette left in the pan. I looked up at her, surprised by her sudden immobility. As usual, she appeared to be listening to sounds other people couldn't hear. Then, moving like a robot, she headed for the stairs, still holding the pan.

"Where are you going?"

I roared rather than said it. It made my throat hurt.

She turned round, looking vague.

"I'm going to take some up to him."

If the small corpse of the kid had suddenly materialized on the table in front of me I wouldn't have got a bigger jolt.

"To who?"

There was a kind of mist in her eyes.

"To…"

She came back and put the pan down on the stove.

"Oh, I don't remember, Daniel, it's awful! But I just knew there was someone upstairs waiting for me!"

"There's nobody up there, Marianne! *Nobody!*"

I got up and shook her.

"Nobody! Get that into your head! The two of us are here by ourselves! *Alone!*"

"I know, Daniel! But don't shout! Please don't!"

I thought I'd go mad if this went on.

"Say it, Marianne! Say it again to get it into that stupid head of yours! We're all alone here!"

She was crying now. But I didn't give a damn about her tears. I went on shaking her and her blouse tore along her shoulder. Her golden skin gleamed; it had the sheen of bronze.

"Say it!"

"All right, but let me go! You're frightening me!"

"Repeat it!"

"The two of us are alone here!"

I let her go. But she clung on to me and we stayed like that for some time, standing, breathing hard, with our two hearts beating one against the other.

## 28

By the time we got round to our omelette, it had congealed on our plates. Even so, we forced it down us, without relish, because we were hungry. The fruit salad fared better. When our frugal meal was over, I said decisively:

"We're going to bring the bed down into the living room."

"What for?"

"I think that it's that room upstairs which is giving you nightmares. So let's sleep downstairs!"

She shook her head.

"What good would it do?"

"Let's give it a go anyway…"

I tried to liven things up. I hummed… She helped me carry down the bedding. I left the frame where it was and brought just the base and the mattress. Though the furniture on the ground floor was appalling, I preferred the room there.

We went to bed when it was completely dark.

"Tomorrow I'll get some candles or an oil lamp…"

Fortunately we were saved by the frenzy which possessed both our beings the moment we lay down side by side. Those were the only moments of grace we experienced each day when love filled us with renewed strength and enabled us to live from one day to the next.

Next morning I couldn't wait to get the latest news. I'd arranged that in future French newspapers would be delivered to the village. They would come on the eight o'clock bus.

When I woke my first thought was about those papers. I had to be there before they came because if the newsagent was curious enough to flick through them he might see a picture of Marianne or me and recognize us.

So I got up very early. I had a sour taste in my mouth but I skipped my morning coffee. I took a bunch of grapes from the sideboard and strode off munching them as I went…

It was a mild morning… The blue of the sky wasn't as harsh and a light breeze moved through the stunted palm trees.

I reached the village at the same time as the bus. The newsagent was there waiting for his parcel of newspapers and magazines. He gave me a cheery wave. He produced a knife and cut through the string holding the papers. The French broadsheets were in a separate roll. I grabbed them quickly.

I looked through my pockets so I could settle up with the Spaniard who stood waiting with his hand out, but in my rush I'd forgotten to bring any money with me. I explained to him by means of signs. He scowled.

He was a large, miserly man who probably slept with his wallet under the pillow. Although I'd tipped him generously with the hundred-peseta note I'd given him the night before, he had no intention of letting me walk away with the newspapers without paying.

That put me in a vile temper. I called him all sorts of names— in French, of course—but anger is an international emotion and he wrapped himself in a cloak of outraged dignity. He snatched the papers out of my hands. I had just enough time to glimpse my name in a caption. If my face appeared above it, I was lost.

But even discounting that, we were already in great danger. Now that my identity had been discovered, it would soon come out that I was in Spain and enquiries would…

I gave a start. I was forgetting one essential fact: these newspapers, which seemed so fresh to me because they'd arrived that morning, dated from the day before yesterday... Phones worked much faster than they did.

At the very moment I was stamping my foot in a village square, the Spanish police were already looking for me.

I had no idea what to do or where to go. We were on foot... Still, there was one solution: buy a lot of provisions and head for the hills. But was that really the answer? Could I hope to live the life of a hunted animal with Marianne indefinitely?

I had reached this point in this survey of my prospects when my eye was caught by a black car which arrived in a cloud of dust. It was a pre-war, very battered old Renault. It had a special Spanish number plate. It pulled up with a wailing screech of brakes outside the village bar. Inside were two *carabineros* in uniform and two men in ordinary clothes. Cops are the same the world over. I mean the ones in plain clothes. They all wear the same indistinguishable suits, the same tasteless shoes...

Their unexpected arrival made my blood run cold. I knew that these reinforcements were there because of us. They were on to us. The fat girl in the estate agent's must have seen my name in the Spanish papers and reported me to the police.

The four men went inside the café. They were almost certainly making enquiries about the exact whereabouts of the villa. They'd be told. They'd get back into their car and be at the villa before me. When I got there, Marianne would already have handcuffs on her wrists and no idea about what was going on.

My head was spinning... I was growling and quite incapable of preventing myself snarling like an animal. I wasn't having it. I reacted with blind rage, just as I had on that first night on the road, when I'd cursed fate on realizing I wasn't going to avoid the collision.

Then the bus started to move. That lumbering bus went past the villa. I started running after it, waving my arms. But I'd set off fifty metres from it and there was no real chance that I'd catch up with it.

Fortunately, an old man with a donkey cart was blocking the road just where the village ended. It forced the bus to pull up... I took off as fast as I could, high-stepping, my legs pumping hard... I saw the distance shortening between the bus and me. The driver blew his horn as if his life depended on it and the old man pulled over to let him pass. The driver engaged first gear and the vehicle started to move. Giving it all I had, I jumped, rose clear off the ground, held out both hands and grabbed the metal ladder fixed to the back of the lumbering bus. My legs dragged along the ground. I didn't have the necessary strength to pull myself up onto it... Fortunately, the bus stopped again to avoid a pig. I managed to get one foot on the lowest rung... Then we were off again... Breathing hard, I looked behind me. The village was growing smaller in the sunshine and the road remained deserted and still except for the great serpent of dust writhing in our wake.

I thought the villa was farther away from the village than it actually was. With my face pressed against the back of the bus, I suddenly saw it flash past on my right.

The bus was now travelling quite fast. I threw myself off backwards... An agonizing pain stabbed at a twisted ankle... But I didn't give a damn... Nothing was going to stop me walking... I ran to the house. There was no sensation in my right leg. Instead, there was a red-hot iron which was being forced deeper and deeper into my body.

I went through the door. Marianne was up. She was wearing blue shorts and a white towelling tabard. Her hair was tied up in a knot on the top of her head. She was balancing a bowl of *café au lait* on a plate and was heading for the stairs.

I called her name in a hoarse whisper, because my voice could scarcely travel up through my throat which had been left red-raw by the superhuman effort I'd just made.

"Marianne!"

She didn't turn round and set her foot on the first step.

"For God's sake, Marianne! Listen to me!"

Now she turned. Her eyes were dead, like the eyes of a medium in a trance.

Dammit to blazes, there was no time for this! I had to get my cash, grab her by the hand and drag her through the rocks towards the horizon of arbutus and dwarf oaks where we could hide.

"Listen, Marianne!"

It seemed she recognized my voice across a limitless, frozen void.

"Oh, it's you, Daniel!"

"Yes, it's me!"

"I thought it was Monsieur Bridon. I got a fright…"

My heart almost stopped… It had happened: she was beginning to revert to her former life.

"Come here! Put that bowl down and let's get out of here!"

My leg was hurting now, hurting so badly that it brought tears to my eyes.

"No, I'm going upstairs with the baby's breakfast!"

She started up the stairs… I saw her go up one stair, two stairs, ten stairs… I heard her open the door…

She gave a shriek and the bowl of coffee shattered on the floor. I rushed to the stairs. I hung on to the banister, using it to pull myself up… Finally I reached the landing. At that moment, I heard the Renault pull up in a screech of brakes. Outside the front door, car doors slammed.

I stepped into the bedroom. Marianne was standing quite still, gazing into an empty corner. She was as white as a sheet.

There was a knock on the front door… In the dark recess of the brick fireplace I saw the gleam of a very handsome wrought-brass poker. I grabbed it by the shaft. I made sure I had a firm grip on it, turned and stood behind Marianne. I stared at the back of her neck which was as delicate and downy as a rare bloom. I was mesmerized… Downstairs, the knocking grew louder… I raised the poker. No, they wouldn't arrest her!… She wouldn't sink back into her swamp of slime and blood! Never!

My arm swept down… There was a sound as of a tyre running over a violin case… Marianne fell to her knees, her head thrust forward… Then she slumped and measured her length on the floor.

I dragged myself out onto the landing and leant over the banister. They were looking up; I saw their tanned faces, bristling moustaches, their eyes black and staring, their antiquated pistols…

"You can come up," I whispered. "She's here!"

# 29

*One day, long afterwards, after my stay in hospital, the examining magistrate called me into his office.*

*When I heard that Marianne hadn't died after I'd hit her with the poker, I'd set down on paper the preceding account to help with her defence.*

*The magistrate told his secretary to bring in "the accused, Renard". I saw her again between two policemen. Only it wasn't my Marianne, but another one entirely—the original, the child-killer, as the newspapers called her. She was wearing a little black two-piece suit which emphasized her paleness. Her hair was drawn back and she still had a medical dressing on the back of her head. Her expression was fixed, cold, calculating. She looked at me calmly, with evident curiosity.*

*"Do you recognize Daniel Mermet?" asked the magistrate.*

*She looked at me, her head slightly to one side.*

*"No, sir."*

*"But this is the man you were with in Spain!"*

*"If you say so."*

*I could see that none of this meant anything to her... When I'd struck her to set her free, far away, in the villa, all I'd succeeded in doing was to reconnect her with her previous life... Our life together had been entirely wiped from her memory... That blow with the poker had succeeded in killing only our love...*

*"Marianne," I stammered. "Don't you remember me?"*

*"No."*

*"But, Marianne!"*

*"That's enough," the magistrate broke in. "Take the accused away..."*

*Before she went, she again looked carefully at me, out of curiosity.*

"I love you!" I cried… "I'll always love you, Marianne, I'll wait for you and…"

The clerk of the court had already ushered her out. I was left alone with the examining magistrate. He shook a box of cachous into his cupped hand.

"What do you make of her now?"

I was incapable of giving him an answer. He understood, got up and opened the window to fill an awkward moment. The sun was shining over Versailles. Two swallows shaped like arrows chased each other across the blue sky.

Then, though I didn't understand why, I began to weep over the love they had for each other.

———

# ▼ Did you know?

One of France's most prolific and popular post-war writers, Frédéric Dard wrote no fewer than 284 thrillers over his career, selling more than 200 million copies in France alone. The actual number of titles he authored is under dispute, as he wrote under at least 17 different aliases (including the wonderful Cornel Milk and l'Ange Noir).

Dard's most famous creation was San-Antonio, a James Bond-esque French secret agent, whose enormously popular adventures appeared under the San-Antonio pen name between 1949 and 2001. The thriller in your hands, however, is one of Dard's "novels of the night" – a run of stand-alone, dark psychological thrillers written by Dard in his prime, and considered by many to be his best work.

Dard was greatly influenced by the renowned Georges Simenon. A mutual respect developed between the two, and eventually Simenon agreed to let Dard adapt one of his books for the stage in 1950. Dard was also a famous inventor of words – in fact, he dreamt up so many words and phrases in his lifetime that a special dictionary was recently published to list them all.

Dard's life was punctuated by drama; he attempted to hang himself when his first marriage ended, and in 1983 his daughter was kidnapped and held prisoner for 55 hours before being ransomed back to him for 2 million francs. He admitted afterwards that the experience traumatised him for ever, but he nonetheless used it as material for one of his later novels. This was typical of Dard, who drew heavily on his own life to fuel his extraordinary output of three to five novels every year. In fact, when contemplating his own death, Dard said his one regret was that he would not be able to write about it.

## AVAILABLE AND COMING SOON
## FROM PUSHKIN VERTIGO

### Jonathan Ames

*You Were Never Really Here*

### Augusto De Angelis

*The Murdered Banker*
*The Mystery of the Three Orchids*
*The Hotel of the Three Roses*

### María Angélica Bosco

*Death Going Down*

### Piero Chiara

*The Disappearance of Signora Giulia*

### Frédéric Dard

*Bird in a Cage*
*The Wicked Go to Hell*
*Crush*
*The Executioner Weeps*
*The King of Fools*
*The Gravediggers' Bread*

### Friedrich Dürrenmatt

*The Pledge*
*The Execution of Justice*
*Suspicion*
*The Judge and His Hangman*

### Martin Holmén

*Clinch*
*Down for the Count*

### Alexander Lernet-Holenia

*I Was Jack Mortimer*

### Boileau-Narcejac

*Vertigo*
*She Who Was No More*

### Leo Perutz

*Master of the Day of Judgment*
*Little Apple*
*St Peter's Snow*

### Soji Shimada

*The Tokyo Zodiac Murders*
*Murder in the Crooked Mansion*

### Masako Togawa

*The Master Key*
*The Lady Killer*

### Emma Viskic

*Resurrection Bay*

### Seishi Yokomizo

*The Inugami Clan*

# ALSO AVAILABLE FROM PUSHKIN VERTIGO

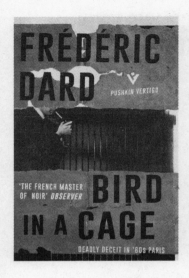

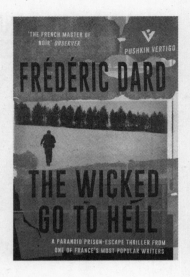

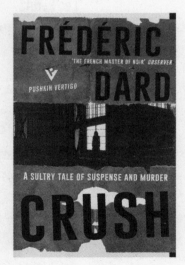

Find out more at **www.pushkinpress.com**